# YOU TOOK THE WRONG TURN

wrongpublishing.com
@wrongpublishing

First edition, published in Canada.

EVERY HOUSE IS HAUNTED

## Editor's Note

I'm petrified of taking a wrong turn. Where it could lead, who could be stalking the shadows, the discoveries to be found there. There's nothing more intriguing than a self-fulfilling prophecy: down the road less traveled is from where your end stems, but who can resist finding out what patiently lurks in the belly of a mistake?

These pieces are some of what you might find in there. They don't apologize for the darkness they uncover, they simply bring it to life. In this way, they become somewhat of a street lamp guiding us down that road less traveled — but quickly you will discover that they, in all their malignance, mean to leave us stranded where no one will find us, to unearth what it means to be taken victim to circumstance, fate, and pure evil.

I hope you love them, these sinister sets of words, as much as I do.

— Lex Briscuso, October 2023

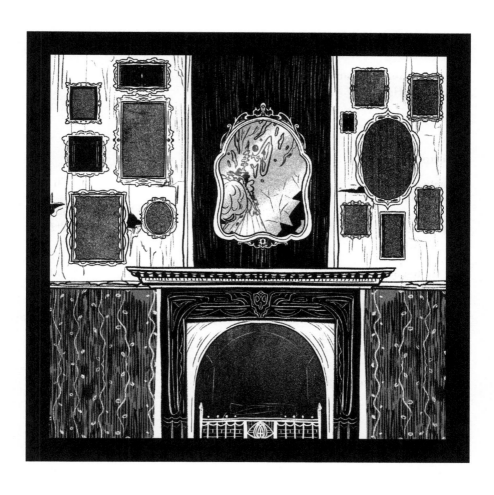

# Table of Contents

## Artwork

## Highway to Hell: Cars in Horror Cinema
### Bronwen Harding

Imagine if you will: a snaking highway, a rumbling engine. Home is somewhere in the rearview, and the darkness stretches out ahead. The lights of the city fall away until all that's left is your headlight beams. How did you get here? More pressingly, why are *you* — the main character of this story — being followed down the road by the all-seeing camera, and the untold multitude of eyes behind it? Marion Crane's paranoid overnight drive in *Psycho* is an undoubtedly iconic sequence, as is the Torrence family's road trip through the mountains in *The Shining*, but both beg the question: what is this doing that a time skip straight to the Bates Motel or the Overlook wouldn't achieve?

We can, in part, put it down to the film-makers trying to establish a sense of isolation. If the gang from *Evil Dead*, for example, are first shown to the audience opening the cabin door, they may well only live five minutes down the road — but we've seen the arduous car journey it took to get here, rickety bridge included, so we know there's no easy out once the Deadites show up. Equally, like a ballet has an overture, most horror films will want to have a slow, moody build-up before showing off the main set, and a long journey through a scenic landscape is a tried and tested method. This even predates both cinema and the motor car: the novels *Frankenstein* and *Dracula* start not in media res, but on a boat and a train respectively. It follows, then, that later stories in the same genre would open in a similar fashion.

There does seem to be something particular about the car, though; not just as a literary device used with specific authorial intent, but as a cultural object in the oral tradition. The folklorist Jan Harold Brunvand describes many urban legends (of note: 'The Hook Man,' 'Killer in the Backseat,' 'The Vanishing Hitchhiker,') which prioritise the car as the locus of horror. Perhaps these stories, most commonly shared between teenagers, reflect the newfound freedom and independence that comes with a driver's licence—made only more exciting by the frisson of danger these mythologies impart. There may be some overlap as well with the horror stories told to classrooms to encourage road safety: most people remember wincing through lectures on drink-driving and seatbelt usage, often accompanied by a paramedic's "worst case I ever saw." The one I heard involved a woman's face coming clean off, and I still don't know if it was true.

Cars can often be used as a driving force for the plot, pun intended, and the momentum brought by a fast-moving vehicle provides a compelling way for a story to take a sudden turn for the worse. In a similar fashion to *Psycho* (and, like *Psycho,* adapted from a novel published in 1959), *The Haunting* uses Eleanor Lance's long drive to Hill House as an exercise in characterisation; the anxious voiceover overlaying footage of Nell in the driver's seat with the landscape rolling past creates a portrait of a character in flux, with no fixed sense of identity. It also foreshadows the ending, in which Nell, now subsumed into the identity of the house, decides to crash her car into a tree rather than leave its grounds. In a more recent example, the most infamous scene in Ari Aster's *Hereditary* shows 13-year-old Charlie sticking her head out the window of her brother's car and being promptly decapitated by a telephone pole. Aster described wanting the film 'to feel like [it] was coming apart at the seams,' and this frenetic sense of disaster is encapsulated by the shocking velocity of Charlie's death—lots of films feature a heavy weapon swinging towards someone's head, but there's something so much worse about hurtling face-first into a stationary object at 50 miles an hour. There's more to this scene than shock-and-awe violence, there's also a slower, creeping sense of dread. For the rest of the film, we see the stomach-turning trauma faced by Charlie's brother Peter— it may have been a horrific, unforeseeable accident, but Peter was behind the wheel, and nobody will let him forget it.

Additionally, from a technical standpoint, using a car as the focal point of a scene creates opportunities for some difficult-to-execute but visually compelling camerawork; a clever filmmaker can use the boxy lines of a car window to frame their shots. A medium close-up with the camera just in front of the windshield can be used to insulate and isolate a character from the scenery by showing the frame of the car boxing them in. As aforementioned, this exact shot is used to great effect in both *Psycho* and *The Haunting*. Similarly, a shot from inside the car can obfuscate the surroundings—the opening scene of *Suspiria*, for example, uses the contrast between the visually legible interior of Suzy's taxi and the dark, stormy exterior to create a brief shot of a screaming face (that of director Dario Argento) reflected in the window.

The car can also be an important visual signifier in its own right; some cameras will treat their character's car as a character in their own right, and will imbue certain cars with what feminist theorist Laura Mulvey calls 'to-be-looked-at-ness.' Few examples of this are as on the nose as John Carpenter's adaptation of *Christine*, where the titular vehicle is so divorced from her function as transport that she seems more like a pin-up girl who happens to be car-shaped. In her seminal text *Men, Women, and Chainsaws*, Carol J. Clover describes how Arnie, Christine's owner, sees her as an 'ersatz sex object.' Indeed, in the film, Arnie's love interest proclaims "This car's a girl!" and he and his friends talk appreciatively about Christine's 'body.' Conceptually, the film taps into the car as a signal of masculinity, transforming the weak-willed Arnie "Cunt-ingham" into a hyper-masculine bad boy. Christine acts as his Lady Macbeth, the executor of his aggression, guiding and goading him towards the fatal trappings of violent patriarchal hierarchy.

There's something delightfully mundane about an all-powerful demonic entity targeting its victims via the medium of automotive accidents. This is an irony that we see in another Steven King adaptation, *Pet Sematary*, where it becomes clear that a cursed graveyard is actually a far safer place to let your children play than right next to a busy highway. This is, incidentally, a huge feature of splatterpunk fiction, which rose to prominence during the 80s and 90s. These works often feature ghosts, demons, and haunted houses, but only ever as a pretext for the all-too-realistic guts and gore that becomes the text's main focal point.

Cars, and other heavy machinery, do have a way of making horror much more visceral. The opening narration of *The Texas Chain Saw Massacre* describes the film as 'an idyllic afternoon drive [that] became a nightmare,' where cars are so present in the imagery and symbolism that the theorist Chuck Jackson argues that the entire film is a metaphor for the USA's imperialist attitude to the extraction of crude oil. Between news bulletins on the radio, oil tankers speeding past, and the gas station where, having run out of petrol, the proprietor sells barbecued human flesh, the socio-economic weight of the car is inescapable. The cannibal family's scrapyard fills the screen with rusted, tetanus-covered metal, making the landscape itself sharp and hostile, and characterising a vision of rural Americana in a state of disrepair.

Slashers in less isolated settings have their fair share of car imagery, too. There are a good number of short-range car journeys in *Halloween,* ranging in tone from the comedic scene of Laurie and Annie trying to dispel the smell of cannabis from Annie's car before talking to Sheriff Brackett, to the tense sequence of Michael Myers stealing Dr Loomis' station wagon to return to Haddonfield, despite being assumed to be physically and mentally incapable of driving. For a film primarily concerned with the home (so much so that it's the tagline on the poster) *Halloween* is full of cars. Loomis and Brackett spend most of the film looking in the wrong place until they find the abandoned stolen car, which the audience sees drive past them without their noticing earlier in the film, and Michael spends most of the film wearing a mechanic's uniform, including when he strangles Annie from the backseat of the same car we saw her and Laurie smoking in at the start. *Scream*, being so thoroughly influenced by *Halloween*, is similar in this regard — the film is filled with linger-ing shots of teens driving around Woodsboro, and Officer Dewey spends a good chunk of the climax drawn away from the house to hunt for Mr Prescott's car. Cars feature heavily in the kills, too: Tatum's body is left on display in the garage, and the corpse of Gail's cameraman falls from the roof of her truck onto the windshield as she tries to escape. Unlike *Chain Saw*, these images aren't necessarily curated to inform an analogy or theme, but rather to charac-terise their settings as normal American suburbia, where driving is a sacred mark of identity and individualism. A key feature of the slasher flick lies in undermining the concept of the respectable all-American town, so it follows that the image of the privately owned-automobile, that ultimate signifier of respectability and personal success, needs must be made uncanny and unset-tling.

Let's return to the question I asked at the beginning: *why does the story start here?* I believe it comes back to that issue of autonomy — more specific than the autonomy of unsupervised teenagers or roving serial killers, the es-tablishing shot of a car rolling towards its destination implies a level of unwit-ting culpability from the driver. In *Psycho*, or *The Shining*, or *Evil Dead* and its many descendants, before we even know what horrors are in store, we know that the protagonists started their engine, put both hands on the wheel and drove themselves directly into Hell, ignoring all the warning signs on the way. After seeing the characters head towards fate with their foot pressed down on the accelerator, all the ensuing horror comes with the knowledge that they could've avoided this — if only they hadn't taken the wrong turn.

# Tachycardia
## Nat Reiher

My heart's a machine gun, nerves on the trigger. Sometimes I freak myself out over nothing and next thing I know, the barrel's running hot and everything's gone rickety. When I was younger and couldn't control the fainting, my dad made me wear a helmet. I hate thinking about it, because I'm always thinking about it: my anxious heart, tempting the three-hundred mark and sending me down, out, gone. I ditched the helmet when I hit high school and now I'm supposed to blow on my thumb when I'm nervous. Imagine already being antsy about something and now you gotta blow on your goddamn thumb.

But sometimes I feel the telltale flutter in my chest and that's ballgame. I'd rather blow on my thumb than pass out in Chet's car, so I do what I gotta do, dutifully. Blowing on your thumb tickles your Vagus nerve, tricks your brain into thinking you're calm and lowers your heart rate. Beats wearing a helmet.

Chet sees me blowing, so he raises an eyebrow and turns down the heavy metal war crime that's been blaring for the last half hour.

"You need me to pull over?" He sounds worried, but he's not. He's more concerned about making it to the campgrounds on time than he is with me. "There's an exit right up ahead, I can probably find a gas station and get you some ice water."

I shake my head, pull my thumb out of my mouth. "It's fine," I say, and put my thumb back in my mouth.

"You sure?" Chet squints at me, suspicious. Then he mutters something under his breath and hits the off-ramp. "Eh, screw it. I need to take a leak anyway. I can grab you something cold to calm your nerves, alright? Can't have you passing out and shitting your pants all over my car."

Thumb back out. "I love you, too."

Even Chet can tell when he's gone too far. We've been dating since sophomore year, back when we popped each other's cherries behind the bleachers after marching band practice. This was, in hindsight, the dreary peak of our romance.

"I just want you to be comfortable," he says weakly. "Honest. You pooping your pants on the leather seat would be the second-worst part of the situation. You being miserable? That takes the top spot for me, babe. Every time."

It takes him twenty minutes to find a gas station: the exit spilled us out into an even creepier shade of nowhere than the highway had to offer: just Spanish moss winding around barbed-wire fences flanking fields of brittle, yellowing grass. I'm not even sure where we are at this point, just that this is clearly where the citizens of Ass, Nowhere come when they need to get off the grid for a bit. We pass a couple of whiteboard signs baking under the summer heat, the words GAS STATION—UP AHEAD scribbled in discount Sharpie.

I squirm in my seat, swallowing spit that isn't there. I hate out-of-the-way places. Back home, at least we're near civilization. People to call an ambulance for me. EMTs to shock me back to life. Surgeons to cut me open and set me right. I was against the idea of going camping, but Chet insisted, said he wanted his first acid trip to be with me—and the boys, of course. The plan is to drop LSD in the woods and have a religious experience, minus Mr. Christ and His signature party-pooper energy.

Normally, I would take a beta blocker—my doc prescribes me propranolol, thirty milligrams. But I don't know what mixing that with acid would do, so I won't.

Still no sign of the gas station. I'm about to insist we turn around, head back toward the highway and its promise of reunion with the rest of humanity. But suddenly there's a squat yellow shack up ahead with a row of pumps stationed out front. The pumps are dull red cylinders and the creamy plywood front was clearly a few shades whiter when it first went up. The whole operation rests on a bed of black gravel. Chet whistles merrily and parks in front of one of the pumps. My stomach's hot and it's hard to breathe.

He hands me his debit card and asks me to pump: "You don't mind, do you? I can grab whatever you want from inside."

"I don't think this place takes card."

"Everywhere takes card, Maisie."

I hand the card back to him and he shakes his head, clearly annoyed. "I'll just pay for everything inside."

He slams the car door behind him. The storefront glass is so foggy that I can't even see the shape of him once he enters. I try to play on my phone and distract myself with the hashtag of the day, but my data's dry as a dead well and I know better than to check for WiFi.

The backroad stretches infinity in both directions, the summer heat distorting and destroying everything more than fifty yards away. I feel trapped, and my heart starts to pick up, gaining steam. I get out of the car and pace around on the gravel, taking deep breaths.

In for five, out for five. I refuse to suck on my thumb again. I do this for five minutes, ten minutes, fifteen, with no sign of Chet. My nerves rattle and my heart rattles with them. The old thought emerges, old as me and just as fearful: Is this what it felt like? Is this what my mom felt? It's hereditary, this clattering heart of mine. Passed from mother to daughter, wrapped in a blood-colored basket.

*Don't let that in*, I remind myself, but that's like telling someone Don't think about an elephant." My brain takes that sliver and runs with it, past the end zone of conscious thought, spikes it into my brain.

Fuck it. I need a beta blocker right now more than I need a tab of acid later tonight. But dummie me shut the car door and now the auto-lock has done its thing.

Cool. Cool cool cool cool cool cool cool.

I put my hands on my hips and stare straight ahead at the foggy glass windows, daring Chet to make eye contact with me through the opaque dark, but I can't see shit.

"Well, fuckity fuck," I mutter, and head inside.

The smell of bleach punches me in the face so hard that I physically wince. The floors are checkered white-and-blue linoleum, shimmering after a recent scrub. There are a couple rows of shelves, but most of the wares are jarred candies and beef jerky. Chet's at the counter with his debit card in his hand, proffered at the clerk like he's about to swipe it between her teeth.

"Who the hell keeps cash on them?" Chet squeaks. "Look, you got a phone on you, right? I'm sure you can download some app and run this card. You've heard of apps, right? Short for 'appliance.'"

The clerk doesn't react. She's taller than Chet by a mile and lanky as they come. Her arms are pale sticks with barely any flesh wrapped around them and her body's about the same, just a paper-thin frame with a pair of oversized overalls hanging off of it like it's been left out to dry. Her neck is a pencil with a skull-shaped eraser fixed atop it, and her beady eyes peer out beneath a hairless brow. A mess of shock-white hair scrapes against her shoulders, the same shape and consistency as straw. Her eyes flick to me and it feels like violence.

"Cash only," she croons. "I'll accept labor, 's well, but y'all don't look the types to get yer shoes dirty."

"We ain't tillin' the fields for no corn today, ma'am." Chet's mocking her accent, but she doesn't flinch or show any sign of anger. Then, back in his normal voice: "Fine. Have it your way. Are there any *real* gas stations around here? Somewhere I don't have to sacrifice a chicken for the restroom key."

She points toward the back. "Restroom is free for payin' customers," she says. "But I can get you some water for free, if that's what yer lady is thirsty for."

I realize I've been scratching at my throat this whole time. I manage to eek out something small, raspy: "Water. Great."

She nods once, twice, three times, and steals off to the back. Once she's disappeared behind a squeaky white door, Chet stuffs his card back in his pocket and browses the aisles. I don't recognize any of the brands: Nickel Nacks, Pecan Petes, Sugar Mamas, Whistle Pops, Raspberry Red Dollars. Chet snatches a box of Cherry Humps off the shelf and pries it open, pops one in his mouth, and winces.

"Well. These are just rocks." He spits out a red pebble and puts the opened box back on the shelf. "Should charge that bitch for my dentist bill. Jesus. Think I felt my collarbone pop."

I want to tell him that it's not cool to steal, but my heart's still pounding and everything's blurry. I try to ignore the drum in my chest, try to focus on my breathing. Five in, five out.

"You're not stuck," I tell myself. "You're not trapped. You can leave, you can leave anytime you want…"

"What's that, babe?" Chet's mouth is full. He's chewing on some taffy that's probably older than God. "You say somethin'?"

"Let's just go." The words burst out of me like a curse. "We'll hit up another gas station, back on the main road."

He chews thoughtfully on his taffy, scratching the back of his head and looking off to the side like a guilty dog next to a toppled trash can. I used to love those puppy eyes and those big ears of his and that way he frowns when he's busted.

"Don't freak out," he says.

"Why would I freak out, Chet?"

He frowns. "Let's just say that as far as the gas market is concerned, our market is severely limited."

The world tilts and I feel the old ticker flutter. "How much gas do we have?"

"Enough to get us..." He pauses, considers. "About halfway back to the highway."

I want to shove Chet into a cannon and launch him at the sun. The feeling must write itself across my face because he clears his throat and says, "I told you not to freak out. I can read your mind, Maisie: 'What if we're trapped here? What if we have to forage? What if my heart bursts out of my chest and —'"

"*Shut up.*" He's right, though. The old girl's really taking off in my chest and I'm starting to feel dizzy. "My heart is fine."

"It's not your heart that's the problem. It's your brain. You've got 'What might happen?' looping in your brain like a catchy song." He spreads his arms wide. "Look around. Doesn't get much worse than this, right? Worst has already happened."

"Things can always get worse, Chet."

"Easy for you to say. You didn't try the taffy."

"This isn't funny." I press my hand against my chest. "I swear to God, Chet, if I have to walk back to the highway, then so be it."

"Oh for fuck's sake, Maisie. Look. Chill out. Okay? You're not gonna end up like your mom. I am so goddamn sick of talking about it. Her heart only stopped because she was pregnant, right? Her heart was beating for two. And I always wrap my dick, so you're good. No problems."

It takes every ounce of control not to slap his face into the sixth dimension. I mutter a fuck you under my breath and turn away. Chet mutters something back as he yanks out his phone. I leave him there, chewing on his stolen taffy, as I slink between the aisles and back to the front where the attendant is waiting with a small pail of water.

"Quench ya thirst," she croons softly.

I take the pail from her, trying to be gentle and gracious, but my nerves are shot and I end up snatching it from her instead.

"Thanks," I mutter, and sip. The water is surprisingly cool. "You said we can pay you in labor, right? Put me to work."

She blinks, right eye first and left eye a microsecond later. The left side of her mouth curves upward in an attempt at a smile. Sunlight spills onto her face through the windows—I realize now it's the only light in here, the over-heads are dead—and somehow she looks almost infantile. She's a foot taller than me and there's not an ounce of fat on her body, and yet I can't help but see a baby when I look at her.

"There's two stacks of brick out back," she says. "One big, one small. I've been movin' 'em from the big pile to the small pile for a few hours now. Get that finished up and I'll give y'all one of whatever ya want."

"Including a gallon of gas?"

She blinks again. Left eye first, right eye second. "Whatever you want," she repeats.

Good enough.

I find her stacks of bricks out back, roughly ten yards apart in a small dirt lot adjacent to the woods. A creek bed runs along the border of the forest, lulling gently downriver. Rusty tools litter the ground around me.

I have to work slow, moving one brick to the other stack slowly, taking breaks in the shade when the bomb starts to tick in my chest. I could take a beta blocker, but that would mean asking Chet for the car keys and that shit just seems beneath me right now. So I'm gonna move these goddamn bricks and get some goddamn gas and threaten to uncircumcise Chet with a stapler and some old gum until drives me right back goddamn home.

Because Chet can talk about me, about my heart, about my anxiety. But my mom? No. And after that, he can't even lend me a hand. What the fuck is he even doing in there?

My answer arrives, draped in the harsh sound of shattered glass echo-
ing out from inside. I rush back in, dreading whatever fresh bullshit awaits me
inside. Chet's back at the counter, a mess of shattered glass and still-bouncing
chunks of hard candy. The girl in the overalls has her hands around his, trying
to yank something out of his grip, but Chet is stronger and meaner and he
shoves her away. He pushes the phone back against his ear.

"You hear that, Dad?" he shouts. "You can add 'assault' to the list of
charges!" He pauses, pretending to listen. "Uh-huh. I agree. That's a tort. She
torted me. Ten years behind bars." Then, to the girl: "My dad says you're in big
trouble and that you're probably going to jail."

The girl shakes her head violently, so quickly and with such force that
I'm afraid her neck might snap.

"My dad's a big-time lawyer," Chet boasts. He pretends to listen again,
and it takes physical effort to stop myself telling him to shut the fuck up, put
the phone down, your dad is a goddamn dentist. "He says we can let this go
with a warning if you just give us some gas. Either give us some of those sweet
liquified dinosaur spirits or you can be Big Bertha's girlfriend in lockup. Your
choice."

She's stopped shaking her head and now she's just sobbing. She yanks
at her hair and twists the blonde strings into harried, bleeding knots. Tears run
down her face and in the darkness, they almost look black. There's something
up with her eyes, too, maybe a trick of the light, but I could swear that they're
further apart than they should be. Chunks of gooey, bloodied hair stick to her
palms like hideous gloves.

She reaches out to Chet, like she's begging him for mercy, but he
brushes her away. When she doesn't relent, he shoves her away—too hard,
Chet!—and her back smacks against the counter. It's a sickening crack, and
she howls in pain. Those pleading eyes turn feral and angry.

She opens her mouth, and keeps opening it, and keeps opening it, and keeps opening it.

The flesh on her cheeks splits apart, splitting off her face in bloody ribbons, and her lips peel, crack, divide, revealing bleeding gums and crooked, yellowed teeth.

She lurches forward and bites down on Chet's head.

He screams. His phone clatters to the floor as his hands flail and his scramble nowhere. He looks comical, like a cartoon character gearing up to run and kicking up animated dust underneath him. A curtain of shimmering red drapes down the bottom half of his face, his neck, his shoulders. She tilts him up above her, lets gravity do the work.

Inch by inch, she swallows him whole.

She's at his throat by the time he stops screaming, and after that, she just keeps going, chewing as she goes, periodic spurts of blood spraying from her mouth and dotting the ceiling. By the time she's at his knees, the soles of my shoes have unstuck themselves from the floor and I've bolted out the back, past the two brick monoliths, over the creek running along the woods, and into the sea of trees.

I run so fast and so hard and with such stupid abandon that I start to get dizzy and the world tilts. There's a drummer in my chest and he's on coke and crack and meth all at once and his heart might explode right along with mine. The world tilts and spins above me, and for a moment, I think I'm actually gonna pass out. Then I'll be eaten. Swallowed. Shat out next to a Chet-shaped pile of crap.

So I steady myself against a tree and let my legs buckle beneath me. I land in the dirt, make sure to bring my knees up to my chest as soon as I can. But my heart's still going buck-wild and it feels like I'm breathing through a straw. Darkness closes in at the edges of my vision.

She'll be up on my ass soon, so I force myself to stand up, bracing my back against the tree as I rise. Then I shift my weight forward, put my hands on my knees. Standing, bent over, breathing heavy. Best heart-rate recovery position. It forces more air into your lungs that way, gets that precious oxygen flowing. It's all about breath.

I try not to think about it. About her. About Chet. Stupid, goofy Chet who died being a dick but hadn't always been a dick, might've moved beyond his dickishness and become a good person again. I didn't love him. But I loved his smile. I loved the way he flipped that little curly-cue in his hair. I loved the way he always bought me popcorn at the movie theaters even though it was overpriced and he was broke.

Beautiful, innocent Chet who had gone and gotten himself eaten with the keys to his car still in his goddamn pockets.

No car and beta blockers. I have to move, and I have to move now before—

A rustle behind me. Twigs snapping. Leaves crunching underfoot. It's small at first, then it gets louder, and louder, and now I've got my palm over my mouth to stop me breathing so loud. I plug my nose, too, just in case. My heart's no calm monk—I'm probably still in the one-fifty, one-sixty range—but I can let my breathing go irregular for a bit and avoid passing out. But if it's her and she sees me, we're in for a sprint and it won't matter who runs faster. One will fall over and the other will feast on her sleeping body.

She's breathing heavy, deep and strained like you'd imagine a fish would gasp out of water. The high-pitched, southern drawl is gone, replaced by a deep, mammalian growl. The exhale is wind through a cave, the inhale like air escaping from a tire.

I listen closely, inching around the tree to avoid her line of sight, keeping the bark between me and her. Rounding the tree slowly while my heart goes bullet-rain inside me. Like aiming a sniper rifle while perched on a washing machine. But somehow I make it, can hear the sound of her footsteps receding. Then there's a snap far off in front of me, some squirrel dropping his nut or a twig finally coming loose and hitting the ground.

Behind the tree, behind *me*, she snarls. Wild, simian grunts follow, along with the hoofbeats from hell as she sprints back my way. A blur lumbers by me, pale blue arms swinging in both directions, her spindly legs bounding awkwardly in front of her like she hasn't quite figured out how to run yet. The drape of tangled, bristly blonde hair looks almost comical, like a wig on a skeleton. She sprints a few yards ahead of, ten, twenty, thirty yards —

And then she stops dead. Lifts her head upward, turning. Her eyes are black as coal, jutting from either side of her head. Her python mouth hangs up and down, flapping softly like she's murmuring to herself. She's even thinner than before, aside from her gut — her belly is massive and distended like a trash bag with too much crap in it.

Too much Chet in it.

If she looks directly to her right, she'll see me, and I'll be dead. I slip away slowly, keeping my eyes on her as I go. We wander away from one another, her searching in the wrong direction as I back up, slowly, eyes on the shimmering white blur in the distance. If she spots me, she'll clear the distance in under thirty seconds. But she doesn't spot me. And before I know it, she's gone, swallowed by the forest. I stick my thumb in my mouth and blow.

The sound of running water reaches my ears, and I follow it back to the creek bed. I trace the current until I'm back at the gas station, at the two piles of bricks out back, at the car whose keys are dissolving in stomach acid. I could break the windows and fish out my beta blockers, but that would trigger the alarm. I'd have a brief and bloody fight on my hands.

I drink from the creek, splashing the water over my face. It's surprisingly cool. But my heart won't behave — it's still galloping inside me, missing beats and sending flutters up my chest and into my throat. My left arm hurts but I tell myself I just pulled a muscle, because this isn't how it happens, this can't be how it happens.

It's a long walk to anywhere. One direction stretches toward the highway, the other going even deeper into this pocket of nowhere. I'll shoot for the highway, follow the road as close as I can. And if she spots me —

You'll die, says a voice in my head. It sounds a lot like Chet. She'll dig her teeth into your skull and swallow you, inch by miserable inch.

I can't outrun her. If I try, my heart will fail and at best, I'll pass out. I can't sneak past her, because the only road back home is a straight line back to the main road. All I can do —

Old, rusty tools litter the tiny back lot behind the gas station. I comb through them until I find a pair of hedge clippers jutting out of the ground. I yank them out of the dirt, unscrew the center bolt holding them together. Two little swords, reasonably sharp.

Can't run. Can't hide. Can't stay here and wait for rescue.

I gotta kill this bitch.

The thought calms me, somehow, rocks me into a gentle, dreamlike rhythm. I'll kill her. It's as cruel and as simple as that.

The plan arrives in my head, fully formed and screaming. Bash the window in and let that alarm go hard as a mother. I won't have time to snatch my bag and besides, beta blockers don't even kick in for half an hour. But I want her coming my way. I want her close and I want it on my terms. I'll hide somewhere, and when she comes for the noise, I'll be ready. I'll jam it in her throat, in her skull, right in her goddamn alien heart if I have to.

I'm still scared shitless, but at least I have something to hold onto. Something to carry me to the end of this thing.

I return to the creek, splash some water on my face, let the cold drip down my cheeks and my neck. It's simple, Maisie: kill her or be killed. Stand and fight, the way Mom fought. She fought for nineteen hours of labor, pushing me into the world while her heart collapsed inside her. She fought, so I'll fight, too. I'll fight. And if I die, I die, and that'll be —

A shimmer beneath the water, right at the corner of my eye. At first I think it's a fish, but then I realize it's far too large. Two black eyes stare up at me, flanking a massive mouth and rows of crooked, dagger-like teeth. A trail of white hair flows beneath it, ebbing with the water, a halo of dirty blonde.

Its spindly arms lash out from beneath the water, wrapping around my hips. Wet claws tear through my jeans and dig into my skin and I'm being pulled under, hips first, into the water.

My legs slip out from under me and I kick at her, the heels of my shoes slamming into her face. I reach for one of my makeshift knives, discarded along the bank. Her face emerges from the water, glistening pale, and those godawful jaws unhinge.

Those teeth clamp down on my thigh. Flesh tears away as she jerks back, red strings of meat flapping between us. I've got one of the blades in my hand now and I bring it down hard, stabbing in every direction, just trying to hit her, any part of her.

She screams. It sounds like brakes that don't work right. And then she's back in the water, a mouthful of me dangling from her lips. I watch the pale, fish-like body sliver away beneath the surface of the creek, fleeing downriver.

And I crawl away, fighting for every miserable inch. My leg doesn't even hurt. It's just cold. I leave a dark red trail behind me. She tore out my femoral artery and now it's painting the dirt red like a rogue firehose.

I'm going to die.

I don't even know how, but I manage to make it to the front of the gas station. The sun's getting low. I lean against the side, gasping for air, like I'm breathing through barbed-wire.

I'm going to die.

I stay conscious longer than I expect to. I've lost so much blood that I can practically feel the color leaving my face. My brain floods with tourniquet how-to videos, but none of them account for the fact that my leg is fucking

gone, that I'm all alone, that I can barely hold my head up and that everything's going dark at the edges.

I'm going to die.

And there she is, right on cue. Walking through the stark sunlight, she
looks almost phony: like some shit from a movie set, rubber suit squeaking
with the effort of movement. Her feet are webbed, just like her hands, and
pulsating slivers of red glisten on her neck.

Her stomach is still huge and distended. Still filled with Chet.

She looks down on me, those black eyes filled now with more curiosity
than rage. A bloody scar cuts across her face, a river of blood running down
her left jowl. She's breathing heavy, and chunks of meat—chunks of *me*—dan-
gle out of her open mouth, slivers of bloody muscle tissue caught in her teeth.

I'm going to die.

Maybe my heart will go out before she can eat me. Maybe I'll go into
cardiac arrest and die clean, here on the ground with my skin still stuck to my
bones.

But my heart is quiet. Steady. What are the odds of that? It's almost
comical. Maybe it's because I've lost so much blood and my whole system is
going into shutdown mode.

But maybe it's because I'm calm, and my heart is calm with me. Nothing
bad can happen to me anymore. Tomorrow can't hurt me because today already has. In a way, I'm safer than I've ever been. I might as well be an old
woman on her deathbed, watching the sunlight dim behind the window. I
might as well be dead already.

I'm not going to die. I'm dead. I'm already gone.

And because you can either laugh or cry, I go for the giggles. They burst
out of me like vomit, involuntary at first, but God, doesn't it feel good to laugh?
It's a relief. I'm dead. I'm dead. I'm dead. Nothing can hurt me anymore because I'm dead. I bow over laughing, a real work-the-abs laugh, hand over my

chest and the quiet heart it houses.

She starts to laugh with me. At first, I think she's choking on something, but then I see that shark-like smile curl up toward her ears and she throws back her head and it sounds like a car that won't quite turn over. Her chest and her belly bob with the effort, and bits of bloody meat fly from her mouth as she laughs.

Everything's dark now, but I can't stop cackling and neither can she. I've never laughed so hard in my life.

## The Greys
### Mathew Gostelow

My therapist said I should write a journal to alleviate my anxiety. So here we are. Happy now?

The first thing you need to know about me is that my therapist isn't even fucking real. It's an employer-approved algorithmic cognitive behavioural therapy app. The mental health equivalent of that peppy little paperclip that used to pop up in word processors, shouting: "It looks like you're trying to write a letter!"

Yeah? What gave me away?

Smug little prick.

Well, now he's back, armed with a counselling certificate, saying stuff like: "It looks like you're trying to have a breakdown!"

Yes. Please just let me get on with it. Mind your business.

So that's my therapist. This is my journal. And I can tell you so far, it isn't helping at all.

#

Okay. I'm going to try.

The problem is, the world is falling apart. People are falling apart. We got so used to shouting at each other online, leaning into our most divisive opinions—egged on by fuckwit politicians and culture war commentators—that the social glue has turned to dust. We're crumbling before our own eyes.

We're disconnected from each other. We're disconnected from the planet we live on. It's literally choking to death while we cut down forests and fly around on enormous planes. "It looks like you're trying to bring about an environmental apocalypse!"

You know what, Clippy? When you're right, you're right.

Yesterday, the International Federation of Flight Authorities recorded 36,000 passenger planes in the air at once. A new record. They announced it like it was the pinnacle of human achievement, rather than a sign of the end times.

Meanwhile, back on the ground, people are dying. Austerity, pestilence, famine, war. And all of this goes unreported—ignored because it's free shipping day on OmniShop dot com.

"It looks like you're trying to buy your way out of a terminal malaise!"

Right again, my chirpy little stationery pal, right again.

#

I woke up a lot last night, same as always. Shallow, fitful sleep, unsettled dreams. In one, my head was inflating like a balloon, filling up more and more, my face distorting painfully as it stretched. In the end, I burst with a loud bang and a shower of glitter. In that moment of explosion I wasn't afraid. All I felt was relief, until my feet jerked me awake.

#

The second thing you need to know about me is I'm a doctor. There you go. I can feel your tiny paperclippy finger hovering over the diagnosis trigger. Messiah complex. "It looks like you're trying to save the world!"

Maybe I am. And if that's true, it's no wonder I've got anxiety. Look at the fucking state of everything.

I work in what's left of a hospital. The roof in the waiting area leaks when it rains. The desk is unmanned. They replaced the HR department with an algorithm, which immediately decided we could do without reception staff. Four out of the five OmniCorp patient check-in terminals—purchased at great expense, by government decree—have stopped working. Messages of passive aggressive apology taped across their useless screens. The software is meant to automatically triage patients based on their self-assessment responses, but like so many of the systems we were forced to adopt, it doesn't work. AI healthcare, just without the intelligence part.

We have half the staff we need, half the beds, half the equipment, half the meds. Every day we treat people in the waiting area because the wards are full. Doctors are exhausted, patients are angry, the system is broken, and the government is rubbing its hands with glee—watching us haemorrhage cash and data into the hands of their cronies.

Christ. I don't even want to save the world. Just help a few people. That would do me.

"It looks like you're trying not to cry!"

#

Something strange is happening out there.

From the minute we opened our doors this morning, the minor illness and injuries drop-in was overflowing. Patients queuing impatiently at the lone check-in terminal. Rain pouring outside, running into buckets through cracks in the roof. (Insert your own trickle-down economics joke here.)

Crying babies, confused seniors, middle-agers trying to juggle them all. The addicts, the unhoused, the vulnerable—people who don't need a hospital, but have nowhere else to go since they ripped the guts out of social care. Everyone sick of the system, furious with each other—cutting queues, pushing, shoving, coughing, and hobbling. People cracking up like the fucking skylights above them. Leaking their anxiety and rage all over.

"It looks like you're trying to survive in a dystopian hellscape!"

The third thing you need to know about me is that I use humour as a defence mechanism.

Midmorning, the algorithm sent me a patient—a middle-aged man, caucasian, overweight, pale, sweat-slick, and bleary-eyed. He had huge boils on his neck. The colour of them was unusual. Grey-brown furuncles, profoundly swollen, concentrated on the throat, but spreading round to the mastoid region, behind the ear.

The patient said the boils were painless, although two of them looked extremely distended—swollen to the size of chicken eggs. The skin around the pustules was also discoloured, taupe, spongy to the touch. I'd never seen anything like it.

While I was inspecting the man, uploading photographs to the diagnosis server, my colleague pointed out a second patient across the crowded reception—a young woman, South Asian background, wearing a professional suit—clearly displaying the same infection. Both had elevated temperature, faces pasty, shiny with sweat, trembling hands, and loss of sensation around the neck, where the large growths clustered.

As I was inspecting this second patient, the first called across the room to me. "Doctor," he said. "I feel strange."

Before I reached him, the man collapsed, limbs trembling, shaken by some sort of seizure. His eyes rolled back, breaths coming as pained gasps, foaming spittle on his lips. I kneeled beside him, sliding my hands under his head for protection. Thirty seconds passed, one minute. The convulsions stopped suddenly, his body slumping, slack and still. The man's breathing eased. I grabbed a blanket, rolled it and placed it beneath his head. With some difficulty, I turned him onto his side.

As I did, the man made a strained choking sound and the largest of the boils burst. But rather than releasing blood or pus, a cloud of fine dust exploded from inside. Almost immediately, the second boil ruptured, another powdery plume entering the air around me.

I inhaled fine particles—a bitter taste of earth and ash. Patients nearby screamed, backing away in fear. The collapsed man was no longer breathing. I called for a crash team on the triage tablet and commenced CPR. When my colleagues finally arrived, I hurried back to the young woman, who had watched the scene unfold from across the room.

She was shaking, clearly terrified, pleading. "What was that? What happened to that man? Help me, you have to help me."

I wished I could. I tried to say soothing things. We would treat her. I'd call a specialist. But paging a consultant only returned the "ALL STAFF AS-SIGNED" message on my device. I gave her water, antibiotics, asked her to breathe deeply, and continued my observations.

The skin close to her largest carbuncle was broken, but instead of weeping or discharging, the split revealed dry, porous, bloodless flesh within. I asked the woman to tilt her head, so I could take more photographs, when, without warning, she toppled sideways off her seat.

Convulsions, rasping breaths. I called out for other patients to move away, give her space. The boils exploded, dusty spores filling the air, dissipating invisibly, into eyes, mouths, noses, vents.

The woman lay lifeless. Across the room, the crash team announced they couldn't revive the middle-aged man.

More cases, more boils, came in through the afternoon. We adminis-tered high-dose antibiotics, but we lost them all, shaking and rupturing on the cold vinyl floor of the waiting area.

"It looks like you're trying to describe a catastrophic epidemic!"

Shut the fuck up Clippy, I'm not in the mood.

#

At home, after the shift, my temperature soared. Internal climate emer-gency. My body trying to shiver-shake itself apart as I sweated on the sofa—a tight-wrapped blanket the only thing holding me together.

Slithering in and out of sleep, I dreamed—fearful, troubled dreams.

Reverberant ticking sounds, deep with subsonic rumble, beating a pulse, thumping at my temples, my fingertips, my toes. Electrical signals spark-ing across shredded nerves, arcing through my overheated flesh, pushing out beyond—into air, into water, into earth—mingling with roots and mycelium, with protozoa and archaea. Overwhelmingly connected. Unlimited chemical

communion. Hurtling at terrifying velocity through an electrical web of bio-
philia. A dizzying enormity, vertiginous unity. The scale of everything. Every
thing. Trees that need insects, that need flowers, that need raindrops, that need
minerals. A hummingbird in the Amazon. A plant on a windowsill in a south
London flat. The flickering of my eyes under their fragile lids. All of it ticking
in time, pulsing as one. All of it spinning dizzyingly together, in a swirling
waltz. My throat bile-sour with nauseous kinetosis. Trembling at the terrifying
mutualism. An ultra-massive symbiosis of all things.

I lurched awake, crying out in fright, tumbling to the living room floor.
I'm crouching there now, sweating, typing this. Wishing for sleep.

#

I called HR this morning, met by a synthesised voice on the line, stat-
ing: "Due to the current medical emergency, all staff are expected to attend
work. Failure to do so may result in immediate termination."

The radio was wall-to-wall coverage of the new pandemic. A novel infection. Highly contagious boils, spread via airborne spores. People calling it
"the greys". Mass panic. Thousands of recorded cases in the last 24 hours
across the UK. Millions worldwide. No effective treatment. Life expectancy less
than 48 hours post-infection.

Roads on the way to work were full of beeping cars, people fleeing—
clogging the city's arteries. Collisions, fights. Human fucking beings behaving
like cornered cats—scrapping and hissing, thrashing around. A spontaneous
bus stop mob attacked a man with visible grey weals on his neck—thumping
and spitting, shouting for him to go home, get his sick flesh away from them.

A nauseating stench of warm raw meat flooded the streets. I breathed
through my mouth and hurried, trying to block out the human remains litter-
ing the pavement. Alarms blared from looted shops. Bodies lay wherever they
had fallen—empty husks, necks ruptured, souls drifting above in grey-brown
powdery puffs.

The hospital was a war zone. I'd only been away a few hours, and now there were patients with grey-brown boils everywhere. Sweating, shaking, calling for help. Some were hysterical with fear, others passed out, some dead, leaning awkwardly against walls, slumped in chairs, sprawled on the floor.

I masked up and moved through the chaos, offering water, ineffective antibiotics, hollow comforting words. I took observations. Everything felt unreal, nightmarish. New cases packed the corridors, waiting areas, wards.

All the time, my own fever grew more intense. My colleagues were pale, washed out — skin shiny with perspiration, grey discolouration around their necks. Their expressions told me I was just as bad — hands shaking now, tremors gripping my spine.

"It looks like you're trying to work through a fatal infection!"

All day, seizures hit the waiting area in waves, patients dropping, shaking, bursting, dying. The air was grey with fine dust, floating infectious. I felt a numbness in my throat, the disease's steady progress. I saw it in my colleagues' faces too — the sickness, the impotence, the terror. We were united in helplessness.

#

Back home, I've just inspected my own pustules in the bathroom mirror. My throat is taupe, squishy under the most tentative touch. Dry, desensitised, as though it isn't my body any more. Three large growths, golf-ball sized, surrounded by lumpy clumps of smaller boils. My skin split wide around the infection, displaying dead grey flesh inside. Painless. Inhuman.

That fearful sense of connectivity has returned as I type this. I hear the pulse that filled my head before. The same feeling I had in my fevered dream. I know it now — I am part of something bigger than my own body and mind, something greater than this human form — greater than humanity, even. We are the metaorganism — a complex, infinite web of symbiosis. I am component and I am whole. The strain of holding everything inside leaves me woozy.

I spin. You spin. We spin. The room whirls around me. The world around that. Spirals of stars beyond. Spiralling proteins within. I feel it all. Gossamer fine. Pulsing and sparking. Caught in a complex web. Expanding and contracting as one. A system in distress, in disrepair. Requiring rebalance. Reboot. I am reborn as an antibody. A sun-drenched warmth. A profound hope. I *will* save the world. I will go on. We will all go on. Nothing ends. Once this destructive infection is eradicated, the ultra-massive lifeform will thrive once more.

When the shuddering convulsions take me, I will feel only joy. Liberation. Elation, as I burst and leave this feeble, toxic form, sweeping skyward in an airborne explosion, awakening carefree as a million true new selves.

# Is He *Really* into You? Or Is He Just A Man Haunted by an Ancient Curse that He Must Pass Off to You to Save Himself?
### Janice Leadingham

In a crowded bar you've never been to, in a city you're only visiting, you order a vodka soda for yourself and a margarita with extra salt for your sibling while they stand in line to pee. You slide onto the pleather-seated stool, your boots peeling off the sticky floor as you go. A 42-year-old song that everyone loves because they used to sing it with their dad in the car on the way to school starts up to the great joy of the bar's other patrons and they scream along to it. You do not, your dad was an NPR kind of guy. Across the room, a man with cheekbones so defined they leave shadows isn't singing either. He stares into his glass like there's a spider, legs up, floating in it.

The corners of his mouth seem too sleepy to form a full smile, and the bruises under his eyes aren't due to the bar's low-lighting. He's probably anemic. When he says it's too loud in here and asks you to take a walk, you feel as though someone is unzipping your skin starting at the base of your skull and that it's her, the you without skin, that says yes. He takes your hand, helps you down. He smells like a cabin in October woods — dirt and dry leaves, sweat and firewood, cider with caramel. You are one foot out the door when you hear your name — your sibling finally back from the bathroom, the forgotten drinks in hand.

### Do you...

- Go with him anyway? After all, you are in a bar you've never been to, in a city you're only visiting! But wow your sibling already looks pissed. (They're a Taurus sun/Cancer moon.)

- Give him your number/other ways to get in touch? But then again, this small town has no discernible signal and the WiFi is simply not WiFi-ing.

    - Leave it up to chance à la the actually accurately rated film *Serendipi-ty* (2001) staring Kate Beckinsale and John Cusack?


At the harvest carnival the next morning, you look for him everywhere. You regret not going with him, and, yeah, ok, you feel a little relieved when your sibling is too hungover to go with you, to stop you from leaving with him again.

Tents with candy-colored stripes stand in clean rows in the old town square. A man sells paper cones of sugared pecans. The air smells like a holi-day. You walk the cobble stone path until you come upon a tent draped in raspberry velvet.

Inside is an older woman, eating a fishy sandwich. She waves you in, wipes the crumbs from her lips. The velvet has really held the heat in and be-tween that and the smell of her lunch, the overall effect is amniotic. For a small price, the old woman takes your hand in hers. She digs her thumbnail into your love line, but you refuse to flinch as a matter of principle.

"Under the round moon, a luminous fish leaps into the air, flying free, dancing—his silver scales are mirrors of the night and the shine of it all. Is he of this world? Who's to say? In the air, he is free of what lurks in the swamp's fog. Eventually, he will fall down to the water with a vicious smack. Proceed with caution. Understand the lure of seeing yourself reflected back in the sheen of him is the fog in the swamp—an invitation for a fool."

You grew up telling fortunes with cootie catchers in middle school and you bought your first tarot deck at Hot Topic freshman year. Your mom keeps faith in fortune cookies and the Mega Millions lotto so that even to this day she slides on her reading glasses to get her numbers. You know the palm read-er is telling the truth.

Unsettled, you flee the velvet-draped tent, and run directly into him!

God, he smells so good. Like a pumpkin pie. Like a weekend road trip in a new car. He laughs, and makes a joke about *Serendipity* (2001). You glow from the inside like a jack o' lantern. He mentions the old castle ruins on the hilltop, asks if you would like to see them tonight.

**Do you**...

- Agree to go right away? Yeah you really would like to go to the spooky old castle thank you so much.
- Hesitate a little? The palm reader was clearly warning you about this exact scenario. But then again...
- Wait. What's his name??

When you said yes, that you would go with him to the old ruins, the moon was fat and healthy and lit your path, and the night felt providential— the possibilities juicy, even.

But the clouds rush in as if they're waiting to see what you do next. Lightning blinks over the hill and you glimpse the ruins. The hulking shape of them like some great, winged beast. You know it's ridiculous, but they feel so very alive, as if they could take flight any moment and that if you go in there, they will carry you off with them. It occurs to you for the first time that you probably should've told your sibling where you were going. He feels you pause and just as he's about to say something, to reassure you possibly, the rain starts and he grabs your hand, guides you to shelter. To the beast.

*This is your last chance!*

**Do you**...

- Keep going? Well, yeah, you haven't even got to the good stuff yet.
- Drop his hand, make your apologies, turn back and head to the hotel room you share with your sib? Hmm, but the moon has retreated from the

storm, and was that a left turn at the Frozen Head Pub? And which alleyway
was that again?

- "To the beast"?? Where the hell did that come from?


At the threshold of the castle is a plaque or a sign or something in the
stone and as you cross over it, the lightning, so close now, blinks again so that
you see the words, "Warning to all who enter here"! But, whoops, by the time
your brain has processed those words, he's pulled you inside. He smiles like
someone who's eaten plenty of red meat—fully.

He came prepared—long, white taper candles for the rusted cande-
labras jutting from the stone walls, a box of matches, and a lipstick-red, che-
nille blanket. A heavy, leather-bound book written in what looks like Latin.

When you come, it's because he needs it to happen. Like his life depends on it.

One hand on your throat, the other begins between your legs. His eyes
search yours, pleading. As if it's your life flashing before his eyes—your birth-
day candles, your final exams, your first dates. Like he sees himself at the bar.
*You* see yourself reflected back. You think about those detectives, a hundred
years ago or so, who thought maybe if you cut off a layer of a murdered
woman's eye and looked through it, you would see the face of her killer im-
printed there. Then, right there, finally—yes—you see all the colors of the
Manic Panic rainbow.


*Did you read the signs?*

**Yeah, like they were a map.**

You think of the girl who slipped out of her metaphorical skin back at
the bar and you want to climb back in that skin, pull it on like footie pajamas,
zip it up. But even if you could, it wouldn't fit quite right—cramped in some
places, slack and pooled in others. You must fashion new skin to hold all that

you are now, all that you contain. Not just the curse, which yes, could be a burden if you chose to see it that way. But you have new wisdom, an understanding that even if you made different decisions, it would've been something else, definitely something... smaller? Tedious? (And anyway, the sex wasn't part of the curse situation. This is not a puritanical cautionary tale. It worked like this —you crossed over the threshold, and repeated the words of the [REDACTED] back to him. Your only crime here is reading some Latin out loud.)

You are the latest in this lineage, a part of a story bigger than you. A story set in literal stone! And this decision you have to make—where and who to give the next part of the curse? How long to hold it so that it's only yours? That part feels like power.

You are the danger and the warning sign, you are what lurks in the swamp's fog.

# The Boy with Stars for Eyes
## Carolin Jesussek

The first boy with stars for eyes got off his bike while I was rummaging through the boxes full of lightbulbs that my monstrous landlord had extracted from the gaping mouth of his garage. The garage was so full that it could never bite down and chew, merely hold everything while the saliva ran down the edges of the cardboard boxes until it gathered in a pool at the center of the room and became one with the dust.

I love the days on which people turn their houses' intestines out onto the street; it reveals so much about them without them knowing it. My mother used to tell me not to look, as if they were truly piles of entrails by the sides of the roads, bad things to look at, so bad that once you did, you couldn't look away from the buzzing flies. "Do not be vulturous," she would say. I remain sure that everybody looks, flies or no flies. It's too interesting not to, and you might just find something to breathe life back into, in compensation for your own corpses.

There were some great lightbulbs in these boxes, the ones with the gleaming spiral wires and the generous, round glass around them. I had already found one and if I was to find another, I would be able to flood my room in warmth, finally. Two years I have lived here now, and it still feels nothing like home.

I've found some of my most prized possessions in cardboard boxes on the sidewalk of the neighborhood. If that makes me a pigeon or a rat in your eyes, I shall be content with that, sitting among my findings: a large green teapot, a functioning printer (ink cartridges full to the brim, can you imagine?), and a beautifully painted cup that broke into tiny pieces when I rinsed it with too hot water after bringing it home. The pieces have lingered on my desk ever since, in the hope that I will glue them back together eventually, but like so many of my projects, this one too remains unfinished. For the most part, the mere thought of fixing things is satisfying enough.

One more box to go through, eager fingers dig in for the last chance of another deliciously decadent lightbulb. The boy is rummaging now, too. I may have let you forget about his presence, but I assure you, I was aware of it the whole time. I'll have to be quick before he strikes up a conversation.

"I feel like I've seen you around."

I had never noticed him around and couldn't tell if it was true, and I inattentive, or if it was a line that just ran smoothly like the grin across his pale lips.

"You take the bus up to uni in the mornings at eight, don't you?"

I do. But most people do, it's a city of students.

"What else have you noticed?" It's meant to come out rude, but as I speak, I notice that it doesn't and could be read as infatuation, or, grossly, as grateful for the attention, even. I try to compensate with a blank face.

But the boy reveals, non-plussed, that he has observed rather a lot about me, as much as you can see from the outside anyway. As he goes on to divine about my inside, which surely must match it, stars flicker to life in the rounds of his eyes. I have had this happen before and while some have been wary of my complaint, I hope you can understand why horror arises in answer to their hope. A stranger on the train, the supermarket cashier who is infatuated with every walking thing around here, the boy who tried to hide in the shadows of a bar, the occasional old man, the boys on the internet. As they think they get to know me, ever so slowly, I make the stars disappear and relish in the dimming of the light in their eyes.

But then the day that I thought would not come finally did, the day I wished for the opposite to become true, that I could make the stars appear instead. We sat right next to each other in the literature seminar facing the professor each week for three months. I made a point of sitting next to you every time. It took several weeks for me to calm the pounding inside enough to talk to you. I don't recall knowing what I said but after several more weeks, when you met my gaze for the first time, I saw that there were no stars to be found, but a darkness in which I saw myself reflected. I know I didn't imagine it. Recognition made the corner of your mouth twitch.

I asked you out for coffee and we had the suspicion growing at the backs of our necks that this was, in fact, a date. Never had I been on a date still having to wait for the fog to lift in the other person's eyes, while mine were as transparent as after a good night's cry. Another several weeks and we were wandering the city at night, shoulder to shoulder, facing forward, plotting a story about an island and how our characters would survive on it. We were treading softly, careful and anticipatory of everything the other said, in my version of things at least. I wish I could show you what this tasted like to me, so that you could finally see the same sky as me. We didn't realize the irony of our story at the time. In the background of our made-up narrative, the world began to close off into smaller and smaller compartments and I, for one, nestled right into it, with you.

At the time, I was writing about a book. Scholars call it the foundational gothic story in haughty academic articles, but I call it beautiful and gut-shattering and refuse to analyze the wonder out of it. The more I told you about it, the more I thought I saw a fleeting twinkle in your eyes, but then the light changed beneath a streetlamp, and I can never be sure of what I saw or merely wanted to see.

Several weeks later, I'm standing in your kitchen for the first time, things have developed, and you hand me tea and drink yours while it's searingly hot. Your cup remains intact. At the bottom of it, a starry night reveals itself. Not me wanting to read anything into this, that you were trying to show it to me when you placed the cup right in front of my nose. I wished to pluck the stars from its insides, dismantle Orion and Cassiopeia, have their parts stick to the tip of my index finger, lean over and plant them in your eyes, first the left, then the right, and tell you "Now it's okay to blink again."

When the announcement came that our compartmented world was yet to get smaller and contacts were to be limited to a single other person, I sent you a text and began stuffing my backpack without waiting for an answer or thinking of the nasty creases in my clothes and impressions. Both our families were stowed away beyond borders that had been stripped of their ability to be crossed. The lights were on in your bedroom, only the secondary ones of course, and you opened the door with sleepy, round eyes, accepted the cold air that clung to my clothes, and let me in. Your apartment, the surrounding woods, and fields of sand became our island for weeks and weeks. We became each other's company and somehow managed to survive.

Days were spent in bed, the pieces of board games tucked beneath the sheets, mugs emptied long ago lined up by the foot of the bed while our bodies remained curled into each other. We watched your plants grow from barely two inches to full-blown bushes that moved with the breeze that came in through the cracks in the walls. We were raising a jungle here. In the midnight hours, it seemed like that forest wanted to make its way into your bedroom and we would have let it, gladly, opening each window wide in invitation.

Most nights were for gamboling about the woods, for discovering each sandy path, to finally stop getting lost or diverted by a window with the light still on and disappear into all-encompassing darkness instead. One disappointing thing that I recall of this time, is that the boxes had, in fact, disappeared and the houses seemed to have learned how to keep it together and their people to value every single thing inside of them, even if they had seen it a thousand times and it was well beyond modern.

In the pocket of safety that your apartment had become, you did whatnot many dared to do in these times and began to peel back the layers of wallpaper to show me your insides. I replied in doing the same as most and tucked mine in and pulled the strings around my chest tighter until my breathing became labored.

When the world began to open up again, cracking like an egg or well-rested joints, we crawled back out reluctantly, our skin still new, vulnerable to the harsh light of real life.

You said you didn't want me to move back out but that you did like a private space to spread out in, that you wanted to invite other people in, now that it was possible again. I didn't want to move out either, I told you, so I agreed to more privacy by sharing the space, which my head did not wrap around if I'm being entirely honest. I saw the half-empty teapots that were neither mine nor yours, the strings of hair that seemed to have grown out of thin air or fallen from the scalps of ghosts and wrapped themselves around the legs of chairs, and once, around my toothbrush even.

The people had taken back to the woods as well, outnumbering the trees, but at least not towering over them. That is a feat reserved for a few re-siding giants only. Dog walkers, runners, and bikers had to be dodged, and gone was the peace and quiet, the nights of wandering, and the reality of a lone island.

One day I came home to a stranger rummaging about the kitchen, asking me if I had seen the good pan. When you introduced her, I saw the stars move from your eyes into hers and did my best to smile and locate another stray hair in the apartment. Another day I woke up to an arm that wasn't yours, that must have gotten lost, surely, and that hadn't meant to plant itself right next to my face. After a few more weeks, it felt like we were throwing a party on any regular weekday, and I found myself having trouble finding an empty seat and even spotting you in the buzzing crowd and its blinding eyes.

The following conversation, in any imaginable variation, had been had for a while, never in a raised voice, although sometimes in one that seemed to have come from very far off.

"It's too crowded."

"What do you mean?"

"It's getting too crowded in here. Too many people standing around, don't you see?"

Lounging on the sofa, smoking by the cracked open window, humming the same song over and over in the kitchen, spread-eagled on the bed, even lurking behind the large house plants, our biggest accomplishment.

"You know I enjoy the company."

On our island, we never found a treasure because it didn't occur to either of us that there could be anything else but what we had already found, and it wasn't that kind of story after all. Now that I have left our island, I feel that it is only right to bury a chest here to say thank you and goodbye and to permanently root a part of myself in your soil. So, on a midsummer night, I wrench free the organs from beneath my ribs and place the pulsing, writhing mass in the mold of dark, moist soil, where it will live on and grow leaves that will vine through the cracks in your walls someday. I only want this to happen when I feel the hole I've made in my chest. This happens about once a month, I will soon discover.

Under a night sky black as pitch, I find my way back to the apartment I abandoned so many moons ago. The dust mice scurry beneath the bed as I stick the key into the lock; they anticipate me before I'm even there or maybe my steps simply fall heavily.

There's a boy inside, a wilder thing, who has made a nest while I was gone. He has painted the walls and is busy changing the lightbulbs. After a small grunt, they flicker to life and, in the newly changed situation, I recognize in him the one who got my insides all wrong that day I was going through the boxes. He meets my eyes now as if he has never not known me. As I see the reflection of a face that remotely resembles mine in the dirty windowpane, horrified, I see, faintly but clearly, the starry glimmer in the eyes of a person that will one day be me.

# Wake Up, Precious Starlight
## Sarah Lofgren

The first sleep's a nasty one, with the cold creeping through. Brush off the soil and let us take a look at you. Ah ladies, remember when *we* were only a whisper's breadth from life? Our coffins secure and strong, the flesh still wrapped around our fingers, and our shrouds unstained? Wait, is THAT what people are wearing these days? Seriously? No, never mind—it isn't important.

Wake up, sweet songbird and ignite your rage, for we'll turn it to good use tonight. Sharpen your teeth, and your nails, too. Though we don't know why you painted the latter blue. Seems... unladylike.

Ahem. Forgive us.

Rise, gentle moonbeam and glide out into the life-after-life. Spin with us from tomb to tomb. Help set traps to catch scoundrels unaware. *You're* no stranger to the stony work men do, and the machinations they set their minds to. You know well what they deserve, when their wandering steps lead them down the wrong road, through the wrong gate, and past the wrong gravestone. Your grief called to us through the unforgiving earth. Glide, I said, glide, fuck, stand up straight, why won't you glide like a magical, mystical wraith? This is a haunting, not a barn dance, and you're a wili, not a three-legged cow with a gland problem. No, we're not nagging. We're helping.

You want revenge, don't you?

Come close, little dewdrop and listen to our tale. Cast your eyes on our trove of mistreated hearts. They were flattened beneath the heels of men, wrung dry in their fists, and flushed down their toilets. Go ahead and add yours to the pile. Dewdrop? OMG, are you looking at your phone? While we're spilling our tale of tragic woe? Why were you even buried with that? No, we don't care what Taylor Swift's new adopted kitten looks like—that has nothing to do with anything.

Look, tiny rosebud, here comes a lad with hands made for rending tender hearts. See how he whistles, not caring if he steps on our graves? He thought he was taking a shortcut, but tonight, we'll lure him into our ruined garden, where there's no path back to day. If *we* can't look on sunlight, why should he? Use your charms, your grace, your feminine wiles. You must have some feminine wiles. Bat your eyelashes. Drift alluringly above the ground. No?

Kids these days.

How are we meant to give deserving men their due, turn their handsome faces blue, if the younger generation is more focused on texting than murder?

I'm sorry, dear spark, we promised ourselves we wouldn't turn into our mothers.

Yet, here we are.

Clearly, we have some reflecting to do. Even the dead must be willing to grow. Let's call it a night. No, it's fine. You can finish your text before you go back into your coffin. But, tomorrow night we are definitely decapitating some poor sod.

## Peach Pit
### Pun

A bedraggled wood clings to the edge of town, trees gnarled and knotted as they loom over the old shanty houses that line the street. A peeling porch swing creaks on rusted suspension chains at the last house on the block, moved little by the faint breeze. If a person were being charitable they might describe the town as sleepy, the wood as quaint, the houses as cozy, but there isn't much charity to be found in the winding back roads of Sycamore.

She doesn't remember anything before the house and its squeaky floorboards and faded decor. She thinks she must have a name, a history, a reason for being here, but she hasn't found any answers yet. There is a man who wanders the house the same way she does but he ignores her when she speaks. She doesn't speak much anymore.

Neither of them ever leave the house. Perhaps he is unable to leave, perhaps he simply chooses not to. It's hard to imagine that anybody might want to stay in this house, in this town, that anybody would choose to lock themselves inside rather than leaving to explore the wide world. He seems an odd sort of man, though, so she doesn't question it much. For her part she can't even seem to find the door.

She moves things around for something to do, to occupy the vast length of time as it stretches before them. Everything seems to take so long, so much longer than she thinks it should. Picking up objects is hard but when she focuses she can slide them across counters or knock knick-knacks off shelves.

He jumps and startles easier than anything she's ever seen and she would probably feel bad if it wasn't so funny. Every slight noise has him on edge, eyes wide in his face as he reaches for the knife he keeps in his pocket, the bat by the back door, the gun in the drawer by the bed loaded and ready.

She doesn't like guns—the weight and sound of them— so when he's not paying attention she slides open the drawer to empty the magazine, sending bullets skittering across the floor. He doesn't speak much but the first time he came into the bedroom to find the gun's metal guts spilled across the hardwood, oh did he swear.

She perched on the bed and watched as he picked it all up, muttering under his breath. He glanced at her once, looking up from where he crouched on the floor, and for a moment she almost thought he saw.

The screen in the living room window that looks out on the street is broken, metal frame bent inward leaving one corner of mesh ripped and flapping out in the breeze. He tried to duct tape the window closed to keep the bugs out but they get in anyway, flies buzzing lazily about the kitchen while moths collect around the living room floor lamp in the evenings.

He swats at them and grumbles but she doesn't mind bugs much even when ants start coming through the cracks in the bathroom tiles. He kills them all with spray and she watches their little corpses get washed down the drain of the bathtub. The hull of her chest feels somehow empty watching them go.

The next day he goes to shower and when he turns on the faucet it spews ants into the tub along with the water, tiny black pin-pricks across the off-white porcelain. He shuts off the water and heads for the phone. She kneels by the edge of the tub and peers in as the ants begin to mill around as though nothing had happened, as though they shouldn't have drowned.

The plumber comes the next day to check the pipes in the bathroom. He finds nothing wrong and takes eighty dollars for the diagnosis. She knocks the glasses off the plumber's face for fun and the man ushers him out the front door and slams it behind him before he can ask any more questions. He locks the door with a rattling click and clears his throat, a wet hack that sounds like something is lodged down his larynx.

There is mud tracked throughout the house and he blames it on the plumber. It would make more sense, she thinks, if the plumber hadn't been wearing little blue shoe covers while he was inside. Her own feet are bare and clean so she checks his shoes and finds dirt crusted into the grooves. She wonders what he thinks about in the garden at night, eyes glazed and hands limp at his sides. She wonders if he remembers, if he even thinks at all.

He mops up the dirt while she fiddles with the radio on the coffee table, switching back and forth between stations and frequencies. He stands, puts the mop away, dumps out the dirty water. He walks back into the living room, picks up the radio, and smashes it against the wall.

The man never goes down into the cellar but she does. It is the perfect place for hide and seek. The ladder down has a broken rung and the ceiling is low enough that most would have to stoop in the space, but she walks amid the mess unhindered. The room isn't large, a scant few feet in either direction. Most of the space is littered with long-unopened boxes and other bits and bobs left to wither away in storage. In the dim back corner sits an old commercial freezer, the type with the top that opens upward. A family of salamanders has made a home in the leaking bottom of the busted freezer, crawling in through a hole where the power cord used to be. She climbs inside next to them, being careful that she stays to the side they don't occupy. They pay her no mind, going about their amphibious business, resting against the damp interior and feasting on slugs and other insects they find in the moist dark of the cellar.

The floorboards in the house are rotting. She can't feel them but she hears the rough squelch of decay under his heavy footfalls. Whoever built the foundation here cut corners, the ground too loose to hold up much of anything. Sometimes they move on their own, creaking and groaning as the soft earth settles below. Sometimes it feels less like settling and more like some beast is making its way through the loam, twisting and undulating, shifting the earth in waves.

He trips over a jutting plank in the darkening of the hallway at dusk, then spends far too long trying to nail it down. The nails stick out at odd angles, plank still poking up above the rest of the floor. He drags a threadbare rug over the offending jut and ignores the iron head of a nail sticking out through the faded wool.

The wallpaper is peeling, a once-delicate floral pattern faded to near-obscurity, only visible in scant squares and rectangles less touched by the elements. Thin nails poke out at odd angles, dark grey against the pale. A couple have fallen out onto the floor, rolled into far corners with dead bugs and cobwebs and long strands of hair. They leave behind holes in the wall, pinpricks that go unnoticed and unpatched. There is a pile of picture frames on the floor of the cluttered hall closet, empty and collecting dust.

It makes sense that the place is falling apart, it's only natural. It's old and worn and he is no handyman despite all of the tools in his tool shed. She knows about the tools in the shed because he likes to leave them lying about the house after he fetches them. She runs her fingers over the cold metal and hides them throughout the house as best she can. There is a wrench in the fridge and a screwdriver under a stained floral couch cushion and a saw tucked behind a shelf in the cellar. The crowbar she keeps close just in case she decides to pull the nails from the floorboard under the rug.

There is a new hole in the wall of the house, one she hasn't seen before, one he hasn't seemed to notice. It isn't large but it is there and not going away any time soon. She pokes at the rough edges, fingertips snagging against the jagged bits of drywall. It doesn't feel like a natural hole, the rim feels torn, like it has faced the energy of tiny teeth and claws scrabbling at the plaster and wood. She leaves cracker crumbs and other stray morsels just inside the hole, tucked away for whatever is lurking. Squeaks and skitters can be heard inside the walls sometimes, but he never seems to pay attention to anything until it's right under his nose.

A sweetgum sapling grows in the unused fireplace, straight and slender with a sparse smattering of pale young leaves dotting its scant branches. The brick of the fireplace is split down the middle and that crack has allowed for the life of this tiny tree. She carries glasses of water through the house to feed the sapling and hopes that it is getting enough sunlight. The air is humid, not quite hot but thick, like being swathed in a warm, wet blanket.

Her friends in the walls have moved beneath the floorboards, she hears them squeaking to match the hardwood underfoot. They get quieter by degrees and she worries about them. The bits of food she leaves around stop disappearing with regularity.

He is sleeping when she takes the crowbar to the hallway floorboard with an almighty shriek of iron against wood, the crack of the board splintering under pressure. The rug has been tossed aside, and the nails tossed atop it.

When she pulls up the floorboard there are three tiny mouse skeletons lined up in perfect parallel. She pushes them down into the soft dirt and says a quiet prayer. The rug is replaced over the hole in the floor, the handful of iron nails left to scatter across the aging parquet.

The hole under the rug gets him the next morning, sending him sprawling to the ground. One of the nails catches him, stabbing straight through the meat of his hand. The scream that tears from his throat is low and hoarse and guttural. She kneels beside him where he has curled on the floor, reaches out to help, but he rolls onto his knees and she pulls back.

His hand wraps around the head of the nail. She means to stop him, but he pulls it out with a groaning exhale and throws the nail to the ground. Blood speckles the rug and the wood beneath as the nail skitters across the floor to rest under the living room sofa. Blood bubbles out of the hole in his hand, oozing down to dribble off his wrist.

He stands, cradling the injured hand against his chest, staining his shirt red, and makes his way to the bathroom to wash the remaining red down the sink. He wraps his hand in gauze from the first aid kit in the medicine cabinet and puts on a glove over it, but she can still see the stain beneath the thin blue vinyl. The rest of the day passes as they always do, he never leaves and she never leaves and if she sees blood dripping from the gap between the glove and the sleeve of his flannel, she doesn't say anything.

Under the broken floorboard the three tiny skeletons are crushed to mere fragments. She tries not to be sad about it. She still leaves crumbs about the house just in case but only the ants ever take them.

Late one evening the kitchen sink turns itself on, she watches the knobs spin on their own. No water spills out for a moment but there is an ugly rattle, a groan, and the faucet spits dark sludge, filling the sink and muddying the off-white porcelain. Earthworms and other insects crawl through the muck. He sits reading in his chair by the fireplace, ignorant. She turns the knobs to the off position but the sink keeps belching up dirt.

The next morning he looks into the sink and calls the plumber again. When the plumber arrives he answers the front door but his greeting stays lodged firm in his throat, jaw tensing and clicking as the other man watches. He leads the plumber into the kitchen, wordless, shoulders up around his ears as he chokes on nothing.

The plumber stares at the dirt in the sink, turns the sink knobs. Clean clear water rushes out of the faucet washing some of the soil down the drain. A worm wriggles as it slips into the dark depths of the pipe. The plumber turns off the faucet, accepts payment, and leaves.

She watches him go and sure enough he leaves behind no dirty footprints. The man shovels the contents of the sink into a bag and tips it out in the garden over an overgrown oleander as she watches from the window. There is a stained ring of brown around the upper edge of the sink that will never go away.

He keeps his hand wrapped and she can see the grotesque bulge of it pressing tense against the blue vinyl. The fingers are stiff, curved up against the palm, useless. Not much blood drips from it these days but on the rare occasion he unwraps the appendage it is blue at the fingertips, the hole at the center of the palm leaking thick white pus. She knows it must reek something awful because he gags and chokes, body going rigid for minutes at a time, whenever he reveals the wound.

Vines cling to the house's outer walls, thick and lush, and a few tendrils have slipped through cracks in the brickwork, through holes slashed into the mesh screens of rusted-open windows. Greedy green fingers race across inside walls as quick as they had on the outside, traversing warped white walls and leaving chipped bits of plaster and scraps of wallpaper along the floor.

The sweetgum in the fireplace has gotten bigger, roots beginning to press outward and upward against the brickwork. There are fracture lines spider webbing the dull red of the bricks and splintering the chalky grey mortar. The pale bark of the tree is mottled, the length of it stretching and disappearing up the chimney. She wonders if their neighbors on the street can see the leaves of the tree poking out from the very top of the chimney.

She doesn't think he's used the air conditioning unit all summer, which is a surprise considering he always seems to be damp with perspiration. He comes in from the garden, wet and flushed under his heavy work shirt, and she flicks the dial on the unit in an attempt to help. The machinery clicks and whirs as it kicks on, followed by an awful grinding screech before the whole thing falls silent with a rattle, the last shaky exhale before the lights go out.

He doesn't seem to notice the racket, wandering listless to the shower, shedding clothes across the floor as he goes. She opens the machine, peering inside at the workings as though she might have some clue as to how it might be fixed. She unscrews the seal on the condenser's drain pan and water rushes out along with a multitude of tiny tadpoles. They flip and flop about on the floorboards as the water is sucked up by the thirsty hardwood.

With as much care as possible she scoops the tadpoles into a shallow glass bowl full of water which she leaves in a vacant corner of the living room. She screws the seal back onto the unit just as he turns off his shower. When he walks out of the bathroom with his hair damp across his brow she is lying on her belly dipping her fingers into the bowl for the tadpoles to nibble at.

He ignores her, stepping over her legs to get to the couch upon which he drops. The fingers of his uninjured hand clench and relax intermittently as he sits staring at nothing. The fingers of his injured hand are tucked tight and awkward into the pocket of his jeans, even sitting as he is. His shoulder is jammed up next to his ear, his mouth thinned into one long line, jaw tight.

It's been scant minutes but when she looks at the bowl again the water that nudges her fingers is starting to congeal. Seventeen tadpoles list in the water, tiny tails no longer twitching, tiny bodies strange and still. One by one she watches them sink to the bottom. When she pulls her hand out, frost decorates her fingertips.

The man dumps out the bowl the next morning, she doesn't know where. The garden, perhaps, little corpses breaking down to feed the earth, water soaked up by greedy roots of untrimmed bush honeysuckle and oleander. He sits and stares out the back window, empty bowl on his lap, hands clenched tight against the glass.

He falls asleep like that, eyes open, and she slips the bowl from his hands and places it in the stained kitchen sink with the other undone dishes. She passes her hand over his eyes to close them and he flinches and shudders at the touch but does not wake. His body is rigid, even in the relaxation of sleep, chest seizing as his breath stutters out of his mouth.

The injured hand is worse when he wakes the next morning, so swollen the stretch of the glove might not be able to withstand the pressure. His whole arm is useless, tensed at his side, muscles straining and shuddering under the skin of him. He goes to the kitchen for breakfast but the milk in the fridge is sour, the cereal in the pantry stale. He picks up a peach from the bowl on the counter and takes a bite before spitting into the sink.

Maggots spill against the porcelain and he drops the remainder of the peach to the ground with a wet squelch. He cuts open another peach and again it has rotted from the inside, pit sitting in a ring of mold and decay, pale bodies wriggling against the greying flesh. He gags, loses balance, grasps out at the counter. His hand slips against the edge of it, too stiff to grip, and he lands heavy on the floor. Convulsions wrack his body, back bowing, head slamming against the broken door of a cabinet.

She picks up the phone to call for an ambulance but the connection is poor, the operator's voice crackling in and out before the line goes dead. She tries again but the phone doesn't even dial this time, beeping like it's been left off the hook. It slips from her fingers, hitting the ground like he did.

Legs curled to her chest on the counter, she watches his body tremor until it doesn't anymore, until he is still. His body relaxes, enough so that his back is no longer bent at an unnatural angle, so that his muscles no longer jump and twitch. Ants have begun to crowd the stone fruit on the floor. It will be gone soon. The man stands, cracks his neck, picks up the phone from the floor. The line quiets as he places it back into the cradle of the receiver with a dull click.

House silent, he walks out of the kitchen. She doesn't follow him. On the floor the ants are gone, the fruit is gone, taken back to the hill to feed the colony. She scoops up the picked clean peach stone and sets it on the windowsill.

A raccoon climbs into the house down the chimney using the boughs of the sweetgum as a ladder. He leaves sooty footprints and claw marks along the floor and she hears his little toes tapping down the hall. He finds his way into the fridge in the kitchen, spilling light from the bare bulb and milk that curdles across the floor.

He finds the family of salamanders in the freezer in the cellar. When she lifts the lid he is lying, belly up and distended, against the smooth interior. His muzzle is damp, smearing red across the white plastic. His body stays there longer than she thinks it should. She checks every day and he remains, the bloat of his abdomen worsening, no longer the result of a full meal. It is around this time that the bugs find him.

Salamanders can be toxic, she knows this now. The raccoon will never learn this lesson. There are choices you make that you cannot step back from. Some mistakes you don't have the pleasure of making twice, she knows this well indeed.

The roots of the sweetgum in the fireplace are spreading beneath their feet. The man stumbles over them as they weave themselves into the yielding fabric of the foundation. Root tips jut through the walls of the cellar and she uses them as hooks for borrowed treasures: a single floral garden glove with holes in the fingertips, a twisted wire coat hanger, a cheap brass locket that no longer opens. The trunk of the tree thickens every day, layers and layers of young wood expanding out and out until the brick of the chimney buckles against the pressure.

A long branch extends into the living room, and a grackle perches on it and flaps about and shrieks. His wings are black, like an oil slick, like the soot that clings to the red brick and leaves the boughs of the tree ashen. Leaves are shed all across the floor, green and gold and brown and black where they have touched the inner chimney wall. They slip against the hardwood, delicate underfoot like crinkling bits of paper. She sweeps them into tiny piles about the house and waits.

The man seems to spend more and more time sleeping, long limbs sprawled across the sofa or sitting in his chair, neck bent at a strange angle, uninjured hand folded over the injured. He rests like the dead, pale, stiff, and cold, eyes open at times but not seeing. Sometimes she thinks rigor mortis

may be setting in, but then his eyes clear and his limbs shift and his lungs rattle out a breath.

On rare occasions he makes it to the bed before sleep steals him away.
She takes to sitting on the windowsill, the chest of drawers by the door, or at
the foot of the bed, feet tucked under her. She watches his chest heave up and
down with the labor of living.

He wakes with a start in the pre-dawn morning, sweat shining his terrified face. He pitches himself to the floor, dragging himself to the rubbish bin
by the door. His stomach heaves and empties into the bin, thick dark sludge
spilling out of his mouth. It smells like wet earth and bile and a shudder works
its way from the top of his head out through the four tips of his limbs. He
wipes his mouth with the back of his uninjured hand, streaking dirt across his
face and down his arm.

In the bathroom he rinses his mouth with a glass of water, spitting the
last of the mud into the sink before washing it down the drain. He washes his
hands, splashes water on his face, stares at the bruising hollows under his eyes
in the mirror before washing his hands and face again. He drains the glass of
water, fills it again and again drains it. He washes his face and hands a third
time until the warm water runs cold.

He stands in the hall for a long moment, staring at a nail in the wall
above a large unfaded swath of wallpaper. His eyes trace down the floral de-
sign, or something far beyond it, before flitting to the closed door of the linen
closet. He swallows, thick and labored, before turning on his heel.

A shovel les against the garden shed and he grabs it with twitching
fingers before walking out into the woods. The sky is a pale grey-blue, sun not
yet peaking over the trees and leaving the wood thick with shadow. She follows, drifting behind. Not for the first time, she wonders if he knows she's
there.

The walk is long and the path winding but his gait never slows, strides

long and purposeful. His hands grip the shovel hard but they haven't stopped
shaking. The muscles of his arms strain and leap and shudder under the layers
of dermis and epidermis. He is so gaunt, so full of jagged edges that she thinks
he might cut himself against the sharpness of them. There is a clearing and he
stops.

Under a wise old hickory is a patch of disturbed earth half shadowed by
sumac and chokeberry and the man starts to dig. He is near frantic with it,
upturning earth with a single minded focus, shoulders taut and tense under
the strain. Viscous dark oozes from his nostrils as she watches, head tilted. His
hands stiffen as the hole gets deeper, fingers clenching up around the shaft of
the shovel but not quite gripping. The injured hand is for once unwrapped
and uncovered, the hole in the center leaking a fetid pink mixture of pus and
blood.

After a futile while of jabbing at the dirt he flings his shovel to the
ground, scrabbling into the hole on his hands and knees. His crooked, greying
fingers dig into the damp loam, pulling at the earth until blood wells up under
his fingernails, mixing with the mud. Insects crawl along his arms and legs and
he pays them no mind.

The hole in his hand grows as he digs. She is reminded of a peach, lying on the floorboards, decaying from the inside, maggots against porcelain, a
peach pit on a windowsill that will never become a tree. Her knees pick up no
dirt where she kneels on the ground, watching him sob and scream and fling
earth haphazard out of his way.

She stares as he uncovers her own face lying in the earth, covered still
in stray bits of dirt. Her head is at an unnatural angle, neck listing to the left,
but otherwise she is pristine. Flushed pink with the warmth of blood, as
though her eyes might open any minute, as though only sleeping. His clumsy,
swollen fingers brush against her cheeks in the dirt, tracing the contours of
her face, the delicate dips and sharp edges of her bones. He thumbs over her

eyelids and she wants to look away.

Wants to but can't because her eyes open. Suddenly she is no longer looking down at him from above but looking up from the grave. For the first time since she had first woken in that house she fully feels, feels the cold of his skin and the rigidity of his bones against her.

He lies atop her in the ground, arms gentle around her, seemingly unaware of her open eyes watching him. Tear tracks streak dirt and grime and blood down his face, and his throat is raw from the screaming, so raw not a sound slips out as he presses his forehead to hers. Moisture dots her cheeks when he pulls away. All the while she stares up at him, gluttonous for all these feelings, strange and new. She feels him move against the parts of her that are still waking up.

He shifts, lying himself along her side so that his nose nestles in the crook just under her jaw. His ragged breath races across the skin of her throat and chest, his teeth scraping against her clavicle.

His limbs seize up around her body, stiffening about her like a vice, a human coffin. His breath whispers against her, words soft and half-formed as he presses them into her skin.

"I'm sorry."

He goes still as she begins to move, a waking needleprick tingle that begins in her fingers and toes. Something wells inside of her, some feeling she cannot identify. She hasn't felt in so long and now all at once her feeling is everything, tangible and moving and coiling tight in her belly, writhing in the marrow of her bones. Her fingers clench and unclench intermittently as the buzz begins to fade, the muscles under the skin of her arms twitching with the sudden exertion. She pushes against him, shifts her shoulders, bones clicking and cracking under her flesh. She tilts her head, feeling it snap back into place, her neck straightening back again to whole. Her arms lift around him and he shudders as she brushes the hairs of his arms, sending them standing straight as his skin erupts with goosebumps.

She wraps her arms around him, around his lower ribs right where the vulnerable soft of his belly begins. Her fingernails prick the skin of his back through the thin fabric of his shirt and air rushes from his nose and mouth. His damp eyes fly open and for the first time he looks down at her, not through. He doesn't struggle against her and a dull disappointment settles in her empty gut. Their bodies wrap together, his stiff and cold and hers flush now with warm red something. His eyes slip closed, breath stuttering out as his heart comes to a final rest. Her own eyes watch as earth folds around them both, planting them like a seed. For a moment she wonders what sort of tree they might grow.

The clearing is empty, earth flat and undisturbed, a single discarded shovel the only thing out of place beneath the old hickory tree.

## Nobody Wants to Be Around You When You're Depressed
### Luz Rosales

Once a month Bev visits her dad in Hell.

She's escorted to his cell by wolf-headed guards. Their thick tongues loll out of their mouths, dribbling saliva everywhere. They can't speak, but they're loud nonetheless, constantly panting and occasionally hissing or snarling. Bev hates them, but she has to respect them; a single glance at their fangs or claws is enough to scare anyone into complying.

They guide her past charred fields that smell like death and through twisting, labyrinthine corridors. There are always screams in the distance, along with moans and rattles and other noises that Bev can't identify.

This time, while walking through the hall, an employee passes by, pushing a cart full of bones. She has another mouth on her cheek. When she sees Bev, the corners of her second mouth turn upwards in a smirk, exposing her teeth: sharp and thin as needles.

Her dad's cell is small and filthy. It's more of a sty, really, with a dirt floor and a pile of hay in the corner that serves as a bed. There's even a trough. There's one window, a tiny slot with bars that lets only the slightest amount of light in. A leash tethers him to the wall, ensuring he can't get too close to her.

Like all the prisoners, her dad wears a black leather mask, with holes cut out for his mouth and eyes. Sometimes, Bev wants to rip it off. But at this point, she feels the mask *is* his face, and she worries if she removes it, it'll be like skinning him.

His gaunt, shirtless body is covered with scars. Some wounds are self-inflicted, others are the result of torture. (A banner above the entrance to Hell declares, "Pain makes the world go round!" next to a smiley face.) He communicates mostly in grunts. When he does speak, his voice is raspy, nothing at all like what he used to sound like.

They don't have much time to talk.

Bev asks, "How are you feeling, Dad?" She asks this during each visit.

He used to actually answer: "I'm good," or "I feel awful, how else would I feel?" But now, he grunts.

Bev has another question, one that's been gnawing her. She hesitates before asking it. "Do you still love me, Dad?" She simultaneously does and doesn't want the answer.

Her dad looks at her for a second, then turns away without answering. He doesn't have legs — back when he was still intelligible, he often said, "Those bastards took my fucking legs" — so he drags himself to the far end of the cell. He stares at the wall, leans in close and licks it.

For the remainder of the visit, neither of them speak. Bev watches him roll around in the dirt. She should be used to this by now, but it always hurts seeing her dad in such a state.

Visiting is a waste of time, Bev knows. Her aunt tells her she shouldn't even bother. The man in that cell is no longer her father, stopped being her father the second he committed that crime.

No one in Hell changes for the better. They only get worse. There is no possibility of reform here, no chance of release. Everyone sentenced to Hell stays there until they rot.

As she's being escorted back, Bev thinks, *There has to be something better than this.*

#

The Support Group for Family of Murderers meets every Sunday in a local health center. Bev attends only because her aunt Margaret suggested it after she lost yet another job. "It'll be good for you," Margaret said, in an overly sweet tone that only made her disgust more obvious. It's her latest suggestion. Painting, gardening, and exercising had all proven unsuccessful.

The support group is led by Malcolm, who's only in his thirties but looks much older; his hair is thinning and he has the most sunken eyes Bev has ever seen. He looks like he hasn't slept in ages, but he's still happy, always smiling to show his thick pink gums. He speaks slowly, and after everything he says, he looks around to make sure everyone understands. Bev doesn't like him much, but he's nice enough, she supposes.

There isn't a lot of talking during the group. As Malcolm says, "Talking gets you nowhere. What you really need to do is dig deep inside and *pull* it out."

Everyone in the group is handed a knife. Bev thinks it must be a joke. They're *sharp* knives, clearly meant to hurt. She's even more shocked by the fact that everyone else is okay with it.

"I know what it's like, having these thoughts inside of you, taking up space in your brain and not knowing what to do with them, just living with the knowledge of such terrible things. It does you no good to keep holding onto them. We must take the pain and get *rid of it*." Malcolm leans forward in his chair.

Bev wonders, *Is it really that easy? You can just get rid of it? Where do you put it?*

"Now, this is a support group," Malcolm says. "We're here to support each other. You can't recover on your own. To recover, you need to *open* yourself up." He spreads his hands, mimicking the opening of a book. "And when you open yourself up, you share your pain, and someone else bears it."

They need to get into pairs and use the knives to cut each other, then reach into each other's wounds to extract the pain. It sounds ridiculous to Bev, the ramblings of some crackpot, but everyone else does as Malcolm says, and before long, they're all stabbing each other. It's messy.

Bev is paired with a woman named Jane, whose blue veins are visible under her pale skin and whose nails are bitten down to stumps. She happily shows Bev all her scars from the previous meetings. "Malcolm's a *genius*," she says. "All week, I look forward to being stabbed." She sighs dreamily and clasps her hands.

Despite Jane's praises, Bev remains reluctant. It's not just that she doesn't want to be stabbed. She doesn't want to be *open*, doesn't want someone else to reach inside her and see her pain.

"You can stab me first," Jane says, sensing her unease.

Bev lifts the knife and shuts her eyes. If they're doing this every week, it can't be dangerous. She's not going to kill Jane. She won't become a murderer, just like her dad.

Without looking, she thrusts the knife forward, and she flinches when she feels it sinking into flesh.

Jane inhales. "Yes, just like that."

The tip of the knife scrapes against bone. Bev pulls it out, then opens her eyes. Jane stands in front of her, grinning with a stab wound in her chest, just above her breasts.

Jane reaches up and pulls the edges of the wound apart, widening it, *opening* herself, until Bev can see her breastbone. Attached to it is a gelatinous *thing*, squirming and twitching as if it has a mind of its own. It's grotesque. Yet it is, in a way, beautiful: it's iridescent, and its movements entrance Bev. She watches until Jane says, "That's my pain. You have to take it out." There's a hint of desperation to her voice. "I'm almost cured."

Everyone is looking at them expectantly. Malcolm's the only other person in the group who isn't bleeding.

Bev takes a deep breath and puts her hand in. She grabs Jane's pain, is surprised by how *firm* it is. She tugs at it until it comes loose, then holds it up triumphantly, like it's a trophy. It flops around in the palm of her hand.

"Now," Malcolm says. "*Crush* it."

Bev squeezes it with her fingers, and just as it's about to burst, something comes to her. A memory, but not one of her memories. It's Jane's.

*My mother made me hide the body.*

Bev can *feel* it, can feel herself lugging a bag containing a small body, can hear screaming, a woman's voice saying "Come *on*," can smell blood and dirt. It's brief, but intense, and all Bev can think is: *What am I supposed to do with this? How can anyone live with this?*

Then Jane's pain breaks, and it's over. It crumbles into dust and disappears. Jane smiles blissfully.

Now it's Bev's turn. Again, everyone's eyes are on her.

A part of Bev *wants* to be stabbed, wants to experience that happiness and peace Jane talks about. She wants to be cured, doesn't want to carry this pain with her everywhere she goes. But that's the thing: the pain is *hers*. She doesn't want to share it. Who would she be without it?

She refuses to let Jane stab her. Backs away from her and shakes her head. "No," she says. "I'm not ready."

"*Beverly*," Malcolm says, like a teacher scolding a student. "Come now. You have to do this."

"No," Bev repeats. "I can do it myself."

In front of everyone, she slices her arm open. There, nestled between layers of fat and flexing like a muscle, is her pain. It doesn't look like Jane's: it's black, first of all, and it resembles a spider, with spindly, outstretched legs. She tries to pry it out, but she can't. It won't budge. It *hurts*, too: it burns her fingers.

"I'll do this." Jane steps forward. She yanks it out so *easily*, in one swift movement. Bev yelps.

It's humiliating, seeing her own pain in someone else's hand. Bev sinks to the floor, feeling as if a hole has been punched in her and she's now missing a piece of herself. "Give it back," she pleads. "Please." *Give it back so I can stuff it inside me and be whole again.*

"You have to let it go," Jane says.

Right before she crushes it, a memory returns to Bev.

When she was eight years old, she looked through her father's laptop and discovered he had a folder full of information about Mrs. Walsh, the widow across the street. There were hundreds of photos of her, obviously taken without her knowledge. Here she was walking down the street, getting in her car, standing in line at the store. One photo, taken from outside her window, showed her in her bedroom, wearing only a towel.

There was also a document that contained a list of things she'd said about her late husband. One sentence was bolded and underlined: "**He liked to tie me up.**"

Bev never mentioned it to anyone. She wasn't allowed to use her dad's laptop and didn't want to get in trouble. As time passed, she buried it, telling herself it was an aberration, a dream.

*Should I have said something? Would that have changed anything?*

The memory vanishes from her mind.

Jane helps Bev up and asks, "Don't you feel better already?"

Bev trembles. "You *took* something from me." She doesn't know what it is, but she knows something is missing.

When Bev gets home that night, Margaret is in the living room, watching TV. "How was it?" she asks, obviously hoping Bev will tell her it was amazing, she's all better now.

Instead, Bev says, "I hated it. I'm not going back."

In her room, she takes out a pack of chocolate chip cookies hidden in her closet and rips it open. She normally tries to be secretive about it, but right now, she doesn't care. She scarfs the cookies down, scattering crumbs all over her clothes and bedsheets.

She can hear the kitchen TV clearly. A woman says, "No one wants to be around you when you're depressed. Turn that frown upside down."

#

Bev had been a good student once, with a bright future. She was salutatorian at her high school graduation and got accepted into a top college across the country for biology. She wanted to be a doctor. What she was most excited about, though, was the freedom: she imagined it would be like a movie. A straight-laced girl goes away for college and makes a lot of friends, starts partying, has a couple flings. When she returned home, she wouldn't be the same. She promised herself this: *You are going to change.*

The day she left was the last day they were all together. Bev, her mom and dad, and her younger sister Sonia, who had just started sixth grade. They went with her to the airport to say goodbye.

"I can't believe you're so grown already," her mom said, running a hand through Bev's hair. She insisted that Bev keep her hair long. It was one of the first things Bev was going to change.

"Don't get pregnant," her dad said sternly.

Bev said, "I won't, Dad."

"Oh, I know you won't, honey." The seriousness in his face evaporated, and he chuckled. "You've always been a good girl. Keep that up. Too many bad, irresponsible people in this world, not enough good ones."

Next to Bev, Sonia bounced up and down. "You better take lots of pictures when you get there. And tell me how the food is!"

While at college, Bev kept in frequent contact with her family, especially Sonia, who texted her almost every day and kept her updated on everything, from the lemon tree growing in the backyard to her own love life ("I think this boy in my math class likes me!")

A few weeks into the semester, there was a puzzling development at home.

Their mother had started leaking. A blue liquid seeped out through her pores, drenched through her clothes, and stained every surface she touched.

Other than that, she seemed healthy, but it was an annoying problem, and a gross one too, according to Sonia, who said the stains were hard to clean.

One night, during midterms week, Sonia sent Bev a video that showed their dad alone in the kitchen. The oven was covered with that mystery fluid, and there were puddles of it on the floor. Their dad went into a frenzy, getting down on his hands and knees like a dog and lapping it up.

Bev had never seen their dad like that. He was like an animal. It was disgusting. More than that, it was worrying. She asked, "Is that stuff poisonous?"

Sonia replied, "Idk."

A few days later, Bev got the news.

Her father had killed her mother and Sonia, then ran to a neighbor's house, covered in blood and that mysterious blue fluid. He pounded on the door, and when they answered, he said, "My family is dead."

Just like that, Bev's life was up-ended. She saw their dead bodies in the caskets and the crime scene photos. They burrowed underneath her skin and haunted her when she closed her eyes or was alone in the dark. In her dreams, their bloody corpses ambled towards her and begged her to join them. She dropped out of college because she couldn't focus, told herself she was just going to take a semester off and then never went back. She went to live with Aunt Margaret, the only relative willing to take her in.

For weeks, Bev was almost nonfunctional. She told Margaret it had to have been an impostor. Her dad would *never* kill anyone. Then she started saying her mom and Sonia were still alive, they were just hiding somewhere. After that, she accused Margaret of kidnapping her and said her family was still at home.

So Margaret drove Bev to where she used to live. Just seeing the house broke her. She didn't want to go inside or even get out of the car. She sobbed in the passenger seat. "They're dead," she said through her tears. "They're dead."

A year after the murders, after working a string of low-paying jobs and trying whatever hobbies her aunt suggested, Bev decided to visit her dad. He was her only surviving immediate family member. She needed to see him. She called the prison, requested a pass, and the following week took the train to Hell.

The inside of the train looked as if it was made out of meat. There were no other passengers, only the driver, a bloated, corpse-looking thing that hung from a hook.

When she got to Hell, the first thing she asked her dad was, "How?" Not *why*. What she really wanted to know was *how* someone who had once loved her and whom she had once loved could do such a horrible thing.

He said, matter-of-factly, "I bludgeoned them."

Then she asked, "If I had been there, would you have killed me?"

"If you had been there," he said, "everything would have been different."

#

In Hell again.

Bev's dad perks up when the door opens. That's a good sign.

"Hi, Dad," she says.

He looks at her. Opens his mouth and moves his lips without making any noise. She waits, patiently, expecting him to just grunt or babble, but to her surprise, he speaks.

"Bev... Beverly."

She stiffens. He hasn't said her name in so long. It sounds almost foreign to her now, coming from him.

"My daughter." There's some tenderness to his voice. He reaches out to her with a calloused hand. "I... I..."

Bev looks back at the guards, who are focusing intently on something else behind them, probably a bug. She's not supposed to get close to him, but she steps forward.

Maybe he's getting better. Maybe soon, he'll be back to normal, and they'll let him go, and Bev will forgive him. Mom and Sonia are never coming back, but at least they'll have each other. They'll be father and daughter again, start new lives and put everything behind them. Bev will go back to school and be successful. She won't have to binge or hurt herself anymore. From now on, things will be okay.

"Dad," she says, kneeling down in front of him. "I missed you."

She moves her own hand towards him, like she's trying to pet a dog.

He blinks, and the tenderness dissipates. He bites her hand, hard enough to break the skin.

#

Bev sits across from the prison warden in his office, a bandage over where she was bitten. The gray walls of the office hum loudly and ripple like waves.

The warden speaks out of a slit in his throat. He has no nose on his face, no regular mouth, only several eyes, clustered together like a spider's. A large oil painting of a man being torn apart by dogs hangs on the wall behind him.

"I'm surprised you've been visiting for so long," the warden drawls. "Most inmates don't get *any* visitors. You have to understand, the prisoners here are violent, remorseless criminals. I mean, he already killed one of his daughters. Why wouldn't he do the same to you?"

Bev says nothing. Come to think of it, he had never expressed any guilt over what he did. During one of her earliest visits, she broke down and told him about everything—her nightmares, the binge eating, dropping out of college, her breakdown—until she was just babbling incoherently. Her dad's only response was, "I'm already being punished. There's nothing else that can be done. You just have to keep living without them."

The warden continues: "He's been very rowdy lately. Hasn't been coop-
erating. And, well, he's reaching his limit." He pauses, as if waiting for Bev to
ask something, but she remains silent, fixated on her bandage. She would
rather be anywhere else than here. She wants to scream at the top of her lungs
and demand *why, why, why did this happen to me, why do I have to live with the
consequences of someone else's actions, why couldn't he have killed me too.*

"This whole nation depends on Hell. Everything" — the warden gestures
around the room — "is fueled by the suffering of prisoners. We've gotten lots of
pushback, people saying this is inhumane, but I don't see it that way. This system benefits everyone."

"Except the prisoners," Bev mutters. There has to be an alternative to
endless torture. She would prefer rehabilitation, though she's not sure if such
a thing is possible in her dad's case. She'd like to believe it is.

The warden ignores her. "Eventually, there comes a point when we've
wrung everything out of an inmate. We've killed their spirit so effectively that
nothing is left. Which is what has happened to your father. When someone
reaches that point, they no longer have any use for us. And so, I've been thinking." A fat maggot drops out of his slit onto his desk. He crushes it with his
hand. "About executing him."

That gets Bev's attention. "*Execute?*"

"Yes, I think it's about time. You've seen how he's been doing. Wouldn't
you agree?"

All Bev can say is, "That's my *dad.*"

He nods. His pupils spin. "And as his daughter, you get special privi-
leges. Like watching his execution in person. Doesn't that sound *fun?*" His
voice raises in pitch, like he's talking to a child.

It doesn't. She doesn't want her dad to die. She can't lose another family member.

The warden offers no sympathy. Why would he? Why would anyone in this shithole have even an ounce of compassion in their rotting hearts? Hell is a monument to cruelty, a place where people get to hurt and torture others without fear of punishment.

He stands and opens the door for her. On her way out, anger flares inside her, and she shoves her fist into his slit. His eyes widen. The inside of the slit is moist and slippery, and when she pulls her fist out, her hand is stained with blood. A second later, a clump of maggots bursts out of his throat and lands on the front of her shirt. She brushes them off, but they leave behind a yellow stain.

#

So far, Bev has tried to avoid the news coverage about her dad, but the day before his execution, she watches an interview he gave, shortly after he was arrested. In it, he speaks normally, even comes off as affable. The interviewer asks about his childhood, and he says everything was normal.

She asks about the liquid. Was it in some way responsible? This is the theory Bev's gone with, because it's the one that hurts the least. That liquid turned him into someone he wasn't before. Others had simply written him off as a monster, an abusive tyrant who had terrorized his family for years before killing them, but that wasn't the truth.

He shrugs. "Maybe a little. But I've thought about killing people since I was a teenager. I just never talked about or acted on it. When my oldest daughter was still a baby, I used to think about crushing her head."

Bev stops watching.

#

She doesn't attend the execution. It would be too hard on her, she knows, though she can't shake the guilt over not being there for his death.

She stays in her room and rifles through her closet. She finds a pink stuffed elephant that had once belonged to Sonia. It had been hers since she was a baby, and she never outgrew her attachment to it, even after she started middle school and declared she was a "big kid" now.

A lump forms in Bev's throat. It had been there in the room when Sonia died. It witnessed her murder. All Bev can think about is Sonia with her head caved in, still holding her elephant.

She hides it in the bottom of the closet, underneath piles of clothes that no longer fit her, and tries to read a book to pass the time, but her mind wanders. She can't focus.

*What were their last words?*

*Sonia said, "Daddy." She* never *called me that, it made me pause for a second. She looked up at me with these huge eyes, silently begging me for mercy, like she knew exactly what I was going to do and that there was no way for her to escape. I said, "This will only hurt for a second, baby girl," and brought the vase down on her head. She was even more delicate than I expected. She died quickly.*

*What about Mom?*

*She didn't see it coming. I just hit her, and she fell to the floor, blood leaking from the side of her head, and she asked me, "Why?" She was crying.*

*Why did you do it?*

*You wouldn't understand. The world will never understand.*

Late in the afternoon, she gets the call from the warden: "Your father's been executed."

"Oh," she says.

"We'll send you the footage."

"I don't want it."

"You don't get a say in the matter. It's our policy to send the footage to everyone, regardless of their wishes. Oh, before the execution, I recorded his last words... He addressed some of them to you. Here they are."

Bev swallows. She closes her eyes, and then she's listening to her dad. His voice is hoarse and slurred, difficult to understand. "Beverly," he says. "You may not believe me, but I... I... I love you. I loved your mother a-and...

Sonia. Maybe things will be better for you from now on. With... without me...
you have nowhere to go but forward."

Bev thinks: *If you loved them, why did you kill them?* and *What am I supposed to do now? Someone help me, someone give me a guide, someone tell me what to
do,* but mostly, she thinks: *My dad is dead. No one loves me anymore.*

#

*Dad, what does it feel like to kill someone?*

*I won't lie. It feels amazing at first. You get such a high, so much energy cour-
ses through you, and it's like for a second, you are the strongest person in the world,
you're invincible. I was so proud of myself. Not many people can go through with
murder, but I did it.*

#

Over the next several days, Bev spirals. She has no motivation to do
anything. She only eats when Margaret comes into the room with food, and
even then, she has to be force-fed.

"Jesus, Beverly," Margaret says after feeding her mashed potatoes. She
looks at Bev like she's a roach that snuck into her house. "You're a fucking
adult. I'm sick of babying a grown woman."

Bev is barely listening. She only hears the word *baby*, and she thinks
*yes*, she wants so badly to be a baby again, to be small and innocent, to know
nothing about this world.

"I took you in because I felt bad for you, but every day I regret that
choice more and more. I've been enabling you, letting you wallow in your own
misery." She kicks a candy wrapper that's been on the floor for weeks and
makes a face. "Your mother and sister would be fucking ashamed if they saw
you like this. They'd want you to *get better*. Martha was always talking about
how you had such potential. She called me every time you got straight As or
aced a test. She said you were going to be a *brain surgeon*." Her words are
tinged with contempt, as if it's preposterous that anyone ever believed in Bev.
"Now look at you."

Bev says, "Aunt Margaret," and nothing else. She just wants her to leave.

"That was my family, too." Margaret's tone softens ever so slightly. "She was my sister. But I've dealt with it. I moved on. My crying won't bring her back."

But Bev doesn't want to move on, because moving on is hard, and it's scary, and she doesn't know who she is anymore. The way she sees it, this suffering is an expression of love. This is how she keeps them alive: by never moving past it, by always feeling that pain.

That night, Bev can't sleep. Her aunt's words echo in her head. *I'm sick of babying a grown woman.* When she first moved in, she would have vivid nightmares and wake up screaming. There would be a few minutes when she forgot what had happened, and she would get up and leave her room in search of her parents, calling for them, like a small child, but then realize this wasn't her home, and she would scream again, because there was nothing else to do. Each time, she hoped someone would come comfort her, whether it was her mother or a concerned stranger who came over to ask what was wrong, but no one did.

After the fourth time this happened, Margaret came out of her room, brow furrowed, and told her to shut up. "People are trying to sleep," she said.

*I'm an inconvenience,* Bev thinks. *Taking up space, demanding attention, making my pain into someone else's problem.*

Once she's sure her aunt is asleep, she goes into the backyard. She gets a shovel, and she digs herself a grave.

The soil is tough. She digs for what feels like hours, never stopping, single-mindedly focused on this task. It's the most determined she's been in recent memory. The pain in her arms and back doesn't matter, and neither does the cold. She shivers but doesn't return to get a sweater.

By the time she's finished—or at least, satisfied enough to declare she's finished—the sun is starting to rise. She stands in front of the grave: shallower than she had initially hoped it would be, maybe three feet deep. Still, she settles for this.

"Goodbye, Aunt Margaret," she says, allowing herself to tip forward into the grave. The dirt will suffocate her screams. She'll starve or freeze to death or whatever else and no one will have to deal with her again. The world will keep on turning and people will keep living, undisturbed by her death, the way they were undisturbed by the loss of her family.

As she curls up, she feels her mother's arms around her, dragging her into a deep sleep.

#

"Beverly!" A familiar voice, coming from above. "Beverly, wake up!"

Slowly, Beverly opens her eyes. Aunt Margaret's kneeling over her, looking more angry than worried. Of course. She's never cared about her. To her, the things Bev does aren't expressions of inner pain, but just displays of immaturity, not deserving of being understood.

"Where am I...?" Bev props herself up on an elbow, looks around. She's not in the grave anymore, but she's still in the yard, lying in the grass.

"Jesus, you're fucking freezing," Margaret says, grabbing Bev's arm, and this action makes *something* in Bev snap.

"Don't touch me," she screeches, twisting out of her grip. This outburst surprises Margaret, who narrows her eyes and scrutinizes her like she's reassessing if stopping her from dying is worth it.

"That grave is where I belong," Bev continues. She tries to stand, but lacks the strength. A wave of dizziness washes over her, making the world spin. She tries to crawl instead, but Margaret grabs her again, digging her nails into her arm and pulling her back.

"That's *not* where you belong," she says through grit teeth.

"Then *where* do I belong?" Bev practically screams it. She wants it to echo throughout the world. "*Where?*" She *needs* an answer.

Margaret doesn't reply. She hauls Bev to her feet and drags her back to the house, shoves her through the door.

Bev falls to her knees in the living room. She gets the urge to cry, but no tears come. *Give me an answer, any answer. Tell me where I belong.*

Margaret grabs one of her coats off a hanger and drapes it over Bev, kneels down next to her. It's an action so uncharacteristically tender that Bev's initial reaction is to stiffen, as if in anticipation of a blow. *This has to be a joke,* she thinks.

Margaret leans in close, until her lips are next to her ear. "You belong *here*," she says. Her breath is warm against Bev's skin. "You belong in this world."

"No." Bev shakes her head. Her vision blurs. "I don't belong here. I lost my place in this world." Ever since that day, she's felt like she slipped into another reality, and she's the only one who notices that things are off. *This isn't my reality. I'm not meant to be here. This isn't happening.*

Her aunt helps her up, cleans her face with a rag. "You have dirt all over you," she says, still not able to hide her distaste.

"Where are we going?" Bev asks as Margaret leads her back outside and towards the car in the driveway.

"To the clinic," she says, opening the car door.

It takes Bev a moment to process what this means. "The clinic?" She's been trying not to think about what happened there. "*No.* I can't go back there —"

Margaret slaps her. Her palm cracks against Bev's cheek, hard enough to knock her off balance. She stumbles to the side and places a hand over her cheek. Her aunt's never hit her before.

"It's for your own good," Margaret says. Any sympathy she had is gone.

Bev stops resisting. She gets into the passenger seat and stays quiet.

Once they're on the street, Margaret says, "You can find your place again. But something has to change. *You* have to change."

#

At the clinic, Bev sits in the waiting room while Margaret informs the receptionist that she needs to see Malcolm right away. "It's an emergency," she says. "She's having a… personal crisis."

The receptionist, Bev realizes, is a girl she knew from high school. Her gaze lingers on her, mouth open as if witnessing something scandalous. This is the very reason Bev hasn't kept in touch with anyone: so they won't see how far she's fallen. That, and a lot of people she used to know stopped talking to her after the murders. "You're being too negative," one of her ex-friends had said. "It's ruining *my* mood."

The wait is brief. Too brief: Bev freezes when she hears Malcolm's voice.

"Beverly?" He stands in the hallway. Maybe she's imagining it, but she swears there's smugness to his voice. The pleasant smile on his face is really a smirk. *So you're back.* "Come with me."

He leads her to that same room the support group was held in. It's more decorated than it was the last time she was here; the walls are covered with photos and paintings, all of them with one unifying theme: happiness. People smiling so widely it looks unnatural and painful. Rainbows and flowers and sunshine. It reminds Bev of a preschool.

There's no one else, just the two of them in a room that is huge but at the same time claustrophobic. The latter is probably due to Malcolm's presence; he has a habit of staying too close.

Malcolm gestures for her to sit on a chair in the corner of the room, and she does, but he remains standing. He's lanky: around six feet, towering over her. Nothing about him gives the impression of strength. Bev is sure that if she shoved him, even lightly, he would fall over and shatter. Still, he makes her uncomfortable.

He stares at her, with eyes too wide for his narrow face, and Bev becomes acutely aware of her own movements. Her breathing is too loud. She uncrosses her legs and unclenches her fists.

"So," Malcolm says. "I hear you need help."

Bev looks down at her lap. "I guess I do."

"I *know* you do." Malcolm reaches out and grabs her wrist, lifts her arm up. "Look at this."

Bev's arm is swollen and dotted with hard, raised bumps. So is the rest of her body. She's taken aback by this discovery. "What the…"

"That's your pain," Malcolm says, pressing down on her wrist. "It's building up inside you. Solidifying. If you don't get rid of it soon, you might be permanently disfigured."

Truthfully, being permanently disfigured doesn't sound that bad to Bev. That's the way she's *supposed* to be: an open wound, infected and leaking. Her outside would match her inside.

"It's not good to keep your pain in," Malcolm says, almost sing-song. "You're like a boarded-up house. Inside you, there's only darkness. You don't let any light in."

"Shut the fuck up," Bev says. In this corner, she feels less like a person and more like a lab specimen, being prodded and scrutinized.

Malcolm presses his lips into a thin line. "No need for such harsh language. I'm only trying to help you."

"And how are you going to do that?"

Malcolm reaches into his pocket, pulls out a knife and holds it in front of Bev's face. A thrill goes through her chest when she sees it.

"I don't want to force anyone to do anything," he says. "But in this case, it seems I'll have to take matters into my own hands."

Bev tries to run, but Malcolm is faster than he looks: he easily catches up to her and knocks her down, then straddles her.

"Don't scream," he says, before plunging the knife into her arm. He slices it open from wrist to elbow, a clean cut. Black goo bubbles out of the wound, pooling on the floor.

Bev doesn't scream, but she writhes as Malcolm inserts his hands into her. It's not even that it's painful; aside from the initial stabbing, it doesn't hurt, but there's a sense of *invasion*, of having something in her that isn't meant to be there. It's *wrong*.

Malcolm continues the stabbing. Bev turns her head away from him, to the wall. She fixates on a poster that says, "Just smile!" When was the last time she smiled?

As he extracts her pain, everything comes back to her, the memories so vivid it's as if they are currently happening: voices, feelings, images, all blending together. There are memories she had forgotten, going all the way back to her childhood. She sees so many things. She sees her parents, she sees Sonia, she sees all her childhood friends and teachers and everyone she had ever known, she sees herself, and in the end, all she sees is a bright light coming towards her, swallowing everything else.

#

"I might have gone overboard," Malcolm says to Margaret in the waiting room. Close behind him, Bev beams. "She is pure now, cleansed. All her pain is gone, and so is any negativity. No more anger for her, no more tears. Only unending happiness."

Margaret blinks in disbelief. "Bev?"

"She doesn't remember you," Malcolm informs her. "But she will learn quickly. She can be made new."

Margaret studies Bev for a few silent methods, trying to decide if this is a good thing. She supposes it doesn't really matter if it's a good thing or not: it's already been done. She simply has to make her peace with it.

"Thank you," she says to Malcolm. "This... is perfect."

She reaches her hand out to Bev, who regards it as if it's something she's never seen before. There's no spark of recognition in her eyes, only confusion.

Well, whatever. Margaret drops her hand back to her side and says, "I'm your aunt. You can call me Margaret."

"Margaret," Bev repeats slowly, breaking it into syllables.

Margaret does feel some dread at the prospect of having her teach everything again—there's a reason she never had kids—but it's better than having to put up with constant meltdowns and hysterics.

She smiles at Bev. "Come on. Let's go home."

#

Weeks later the tape arrives, unlabeled, in the mail. Bev and Margaret watch it together.

In a barren landscape, a man without legs hangs upside down over a giant hole, suspended from a tower. Blood and bruises coat his body. His face is swollen and discolored beyond recognition. For a few seconds he sways in midair, blown around by the breeze. The rope is severed suddenly, and he plummets into the hole.

Inside that hole: a mass of bodies, all mutilated and rotting, all of them dead except for him, he who still moves, who looks up and communicates through his expression that he knows he is never getting out, is basically dead already and this is his grave.

The video ends.

"He must have done something really bad," Bev remarks.

"Yes," Margaret says, "he did."

## Grass
### Joseph Alcala

I was looking for a song when I came across the channel. The thumbnail was dark and grainy, a tiny FaceTime square in the corner showed a face
set in horror. Less than a hundred views. I couldn't resist. I clicked.

There is a brief pause of darkness before an image appears—a Face-
Time call between a man and a woman, both young, around my own age. The
small square holds a woman in a dimly lit room. Her face is partially cast in
shadow by her hair. The man, taking up the majority of the screen, is outside.
It is night.

"I have to do this."

He looks ill, visibly shaken. Not as if his body is trembling, but as if
something unseen—perhaps in the background too dark to make anything out
of—is shaking him.

"I wish you wouldn't."

He sets the camera on the ground, propped against something. Visible
are only grass and some trees on the side, receding into the background. He
lies on his stomach facing the camera. From his pocket he removes, slowly,
reverently, a pocket knife that he then, just as reverently, flips open. It gleams
in the darkness. The girl looks almost as sick as him now, but it is her own un-
easiness, belonging to her.

Slowly, meticulously, he begins to scrape the grass off of the earth. His
movements are smooth, fluid. His hand pulls forward, fingers extending the
knife across the ground, bringing the blade over the earth. The blade makes its
way toward the camera, slicing through the horizon line where dirt ends and
grass begins. In the path he makes it was as if grass had never grown there.
Once the stroke of his knife brings it beyond the camera's view, he brings it
back and shaves off the grass next to it. He does this until the patch of ground

before him is completely bare of grass. The video is exactly three minutes long.

The woman is crying.

In the last few seconds he gets onto his knees, looks down. The woman's finger moves to the camera and the video ends.

Aside from describing the video, I can't really explain what was so unnerving about it. It was something bizarre, unexplained. It was the channel's only video and had been posted a week before. I subscribed in case anything else was posted in the future.

#

I saw that video in 2012, at the age of 14. Years passed. I completely forgot about the channel, vaguely remembering an unnerving internet video — a genre my mind had an unhealthy but normal-for-my-generation archive of. 10 years later, bored and scrolling through my subscriptions tab, I saw a video with a profile icon that brought everything back to me. 0 views. I was the first.

This video was long — just over four hours. It instantly opened onto a crackling fireplace. The camera captured a little of its border — typical brick, but illuminated from some off camera light source. A faint pale blue that the glow of the fire danced against. After a few seconds of this, I skipped through the video. Nothing changed. The fire crackled, seemingly endlessly. I went back to the channel page and saw the old video, 11 years old, with 238 views. So others had seen it, but not many.

I went back to the new video. This time I noticed something in the fire, a small gleam within the blaze. I could just make out the wooden handle of the pocket knife before it was consumed by flames.

I had just graduated college with a useless degree and was piecing together a living through various gig jobs. It was just enough to provide for the solitary life I wanted. These days I barely even cared to use social media as connective tissue. It was just content.

Maybe that's why the new video affected me so much. It and the video that came before were relics of an older internet, one where the inexplicable could be shared. Not content, not even art, but something secret. Something wrong. A side of humanity I imagine few saw before the internet. It didn't belong to the world I was now living in.

I reposted the first video on reddit and elsewhere. Not a single person had seen it. Most chalked it up to the era of Youtube it was from. They found it funny. Still, barely anyone cared to be involved with it. The views didn't even go up by a hundred.

#

I waited until past midnight, knowing that it was rare to see dog walkers out that late. I stepped out to my apartment courtyard—a small space by the parking lot with a stretch of grass and a few trees—and got on my stomach. From my hoodie pocket I brought out a kitchen knife. No pocket knife, so it would have to do. The grass bristling against my own stubble was wet and cold. I was too curious to feel ridiculous. Slowly, following his movements from the video, I held out the blade, pressed it firmly, gently against the ground, and shaved off a line of grass. Resistance, release. There was a strange pleasure to it. I thought of the boy's nervousness in the video, his compulsion—I felt none of that. But I did want to continue. I shaved off another line.

"Um… hello?"

I froze. A delinquent shame surged through me. A creepy man lying on the ground with a knife in the dead of night. Who was I?

I turned my head to the side and saw a woman on the sidewalk—Claire, a neighbor I sorta knew, who lived a few floors above me.

"Oh, hey…"

At the sound of my voice her shoulders fell a little. Only a little.

"What are you doing?"

I exhaled a nervous laugh. What was there to explain? Not even the truth made sense. It felt like something had sat on me, pinning me to the ground and constricting my throat.

"Is that a knife?"

"Yeah. I was cutting the grass."

"You were cutting the grass... with a knife?"

This time I really laughed. But I was nervous now. I had a witness.

"I can't really explain it... It's something I just had to try."

I could tell that she wanted to go. It was obvious I could be a threat. Still, something seemed to trouble her.

"You're not gonna hurt yourself, are you?"

That gave me pause. I looked down at the wrist holding the knife. Ages ago—not long after seeing the video for the first time—I stood in the kitchen, held a knife to my throat and thought about it. I felt the serrations pressing into my Adam's apple and imagined the pain of them slicing into me, releasing me. I hadn't done it since.

Lying there, I started to realize I couldn't move.

"I don't think I can get up."

"Do you want me to call someone? An ambulance?"

I was sweating. The thought of another person—people—seeing me here pinned me down harder than I already was. I gasped out my next words.

"No, please... but... do you think... you could watch?"

She went quiet. I knew I'd gone too far. Without a word, she continued walking towards the building, taking something out of her purse.

I was suddenly terrified that if she left me there I'd never be able to get up again.

"Wait!"

Perhaps it was my desperation—pleading, placating—that made her stop and glance back over her shoulder. As fast as I could, struggling against the unseen weight, I grabbed a chunk of grass and sliced it off the dirt. She stared for a few seconds before turning and hurrying into the building.

The second the door slammed shut, oxygen rushed back into my lungs. I could breathe. I could move.

#

I'm writing all this down to try and make sense of things, but the more I write the less I know. What I did know, however, because I had seen the video and now understood his fear, was that I would have to do it again.

It doesn't live with me at every moment, but it is easily triggered. Walking past a barber shop, blades sliding over scalps. A lawnmower. The thought of slit wrists. I even held a knife against my own, but it did nothing.

I became obsessed with the horizon line. One night I got onto my apartment's roof to watch the sunset. I imagined everything above that line being shaved off the earth—buildings, trees, cars, people. On the bus, I imagine infinitely long blades protruding from both sides of the vehicle, shaving the globe, devastating the earth, driving until all of it is gone.

I don't want to have these thoughts. I would never hurt anyone. It's just I now have this need to cut—to shave, to slice away extremities from the smooth surface. How I long to stroke perfectly flat, clean ground. That doesn't exist anywhere.

On the roof, I thought back to the second video. The knife destroyed. A message, one of triumph over impulse. A strong enough sense of victory to share with others.

But it was too late.

I could only see it as a loss.

# Vampire Radio
## J. M. Tyree

Luxembourg, my Luxembourg, highest GDP per capita in the world. Your highway gas stations are stuffed with leaflets for museums and symphonies, and you advertise a permanent photographic exhibition that claims to represent "The Family of Man." Up on the hill, the modern city with its tediously well-appointed banking havens and fried fish in dry Mosel Riesling, below in the valley, the remnants of the medieval town, swarming with ghosts. They say that everyone Luxembourgish is related to the royal family, well-known throughout Europe as elegant vampires in suits and tiaras. (Net worth: $5 billion.) In the 1930s, their legendary radio transmitter broadcast the first radio commercials from Luxembourg into England, circumventing the laws outlawing advertising on the airwaves, pirating the spectrum for secret decoder rings that spelled out the virtues of drinking Ovaltine. Now it's Malaysian industrial banks and the international clientele who can't meet the strictures of hiding money in Switzerland or Liechtenstein. During my lessons in Luxembourgish—required by my company as a condition of my visa—I discovered that the language is spoken by an enclave of ethnic Germans in Transylvania. I more or less gave up on my studies after discovering that the language subdivides into eight dialects, but I still use *"Gudden Owend"* for "Good Evening," thinking every time of Bela Lugosi's line in *Dracula*, "We will be leaving, tomorrow evening." On conference calls with New York and London, colleagues often ask me if there is nightlife in Luxembourg City. I tell them it's better not to be seen on the streets near the palace after dark.

#

My work is not very glamorous even though it involves millions of dollars. I tend to the machine all day. My back has become slightly curved over the years from this work, and my fingers often go numb at dinner. I think the

screen has damaged my eyes — the doctors tell me that my corneas are warped
and scarred. I need special contact lenses in order to see what I'm doing. The
lenses are filled with sterile water, then affixed to my eyes with suction. I see
everything through the liquid, as if I am swimming underwater. If you saw me
at work, you would think that my job involved staring at a screen, in total si-
lence, for hours on end. From time to time, I hit a key that buys or sells equi-
ties, bonds, futures, options, derivatives, real estate, distressed properties, cur-
rencies. My clients expect large returns, so each press of the key is, for me,
freighted with suspense. I am a gambler combined with a kind of night
watchman on a ship headed for fishing grounds, if I am lucky, or typhoons, if
the timing is bad. To the casual observer, I might appear to be sitting in medi-
tation, my fingers melding with the keyboard, my eyes reflecting global weath-
er patterns, swaying foreign exchanges, and continuously updated news feeds
about coups, changes of government, political trends, fashion, and technologi-
cal breakthroughs. I might look a little witless and passive, my brain slowly
drawn into the screen by an invisible tractor-beam. Tending the machine, I
keep thinking about a man whose job it is to shovel coal into the engine of an
old fashioned steam train, only the bits of coal I'm shoveling in are people's
dreams of fabulous wealth, and the engine steam produced contains the
nightmares of deep-ocean drilling, coltan mines, uranium enrichment, ship-
breaking, factory farms, garment-industry fires, and the pesticides sprayed over
vast coffee plantations. On other days I find myself building bridges and hy-
droelectric dams to power cities and manufacture clean water and sterile hos-
pitals, bonds that pay for schools and medicine and pensions and cheap mobile phones that tell farmers when to harvest most profitably and wind-up
solar-powered radios that broadcast the deathless gospel of rising tides and
lifting boats.

#

Probably you can already tell that I am a liar. I have no doubt that you are able to see through me, regarder of the sorrows of the world. I moonlight as a counterfeiter, stamping out fraudulent cryptocurrencies to be used in real transactions by unwitting victims of cash extractions on the dark web. If I say I am living in Luxembourg City and that I work in global finance, that's not very convincing, but it is far more interesting than the truth. I must hide my real location so that local authorities in my area are one step behind. My addiction is to fraud. In my spare time I fabricate new identities, fake news, invented histories, novel conspiracy theories, made-up persons having made-up conversations in imaginary situations. I was the inventor of Third Life, a place in Second Life where the online avatars of real people had avatars of their own, so that they could escape from the fantasies of the game. In Third Life, everyone is ugly and sinister. There's no beach volleyball and morphine is plentiful. I was the theoretician who proposed that each black hole rips open an all-powerful tear in the fabric of the universe, creating another Big Bang and another universe on the other side. I wake up at sunset, brush the soil from my silk pillow, and broadcast coded numbers to a worldwide community of dead souls and pod people lurking in basements and garden sheds. I used to write novels until the robots took over the creative industries—machines are doing a much better job at creating commercially viable narratives for use by the publishing conglomerates and movie studios. They never mix up their backstories, they always ensure that characters are likable and relatable, and they always produce dramas of moral decision-making in which a compelling protagonist faces a suspenseful crossroads in their relationships. Now my fictions take the form of crimes. I am paid to post the damning negative review of the well-established product by their competitor. I tell the story of rising sea levels and collapsing ice-shelves caused by sunspots or changes in the magnetosphere. I puff the penny stocks on the online forum just before the shares are dumped. I weave the theories that create the impression of a many-tentacled foreign power that, in reality, wields only shadows in its arsenal. This is the literature of the future. The organization that employs me allows my many poison pen-names to pop out of rabbit holes connecting seventeen countries. I do not know the names of my superiors. I recently sent you that letter promising to release your metadata if you did not download a certain app and send bitcoins to a bank account in Belarus. I do not really have anything on you, but I can make an educated guess based on human nature. What none of us want any-one to know, the thing that we fear the most, is for the people who are nearest and dearest to us to find out who we really are. Did you receive my previous message? I'm in your neighborhood, only three miles away, and I like hot chat with older users such as yourself. Please, love me, save me, remember me, hell is to be forgotten.

#

Due to reasons I would rather not explain now, I had to relocate in a hurry, and wound up in Luxembourg City. Here, my luck turned and I became enormously successful as a result of investing venture capital in a foolproof invention that detected bombs and was the size of a tea saucer that could be affixed to planes, buses, cars, and building entrances. My tax returns, which had been included in a cyber-hack targeting figures in global financial institu-tions, had been made public. Their salutation to the world was "Dear Vam-pires." I felt more like Mickey Mouse in *The Sorcerer's Apprentice,* with the ef-fects of global capitalism represented by all those magically multiplying brooms created by Mickey's attempt to kill the creature by chopping it up with an ax. We're in the whirlpool, we're being drowned, and there is no spell and no wizard.

#

My latest business proposal: *Robotics company seeks fiction writers.* We need you to manufacture convincing individual personalities and coherent personal histories for our line of artificially intelligent androids. We build powerfully bright empathic personal assistants, replacement spouses, and mis-

tresses, as well as readymade friends, instant colleagues, and, pending legaliza-
tion, children for couples unable to conceive naturally or artificially. This is an
immensely rewarding world, with compensation in line with your previous
experience as a well-reviewed novelist, short story writer, or script developer
for movies, television, streaming video, or video games. Best of all, we encourage you to impart little details from your own life and memories as often as
possible, for the sake of realism. This, in turn, becomes your shortcut to im-
mortality, with episodes, personalities, and stories from your life living on, re-
cycled down the generations, used to improve the lives of a growing client
base in the hundreds of thousands.

#

My friend sends me her latest video diary from Sri Lanka, the footage
accompanied by her strong musical voice. Everything in that country looks
soft-edged, damp, decayed. Even the trains appear like clay that might fall
apart at any moment. The tracks seem to float and meander like rivers. After
watching her movie, I walk around the undead streets of the financial center,
here in a micronation at the heart of Europe, a capital of capital, a city where I
do not speak the local language and everything is scrubbed too clean. My
world feels prosperous and bleak now. It's as if my skull is made of crystal or
covered in diamonds. I decide that I need to travel, go somewhere out of town,
but the station is closed up for the evening when I arrive on foot. Hundreds of
bicycles appear on the platform, as if they have been abandoned in a hurry by
a retreating army. The bikes look antique, and all the signs around the station
are only in German, rather than the usual Luxembourgish, French, English,
and German. The hair starts rising on the back of my neck, but when the tattered band of partisans arrive, they are delighted to discover that I am an
American. Opening a bottle of dry Mosel Riesling they quiz me in English
about my strange civilian uniform and ask me what outfit I serve. (Isn't that
the question?) In an attempt to make me feel more at home, they break into a

song I don't recognize, a children's advertising radio jingle for Ovaltine. Everybody memorized it, growing up around here, before the war. I've traveled back in time, somehow, to 1944.

#

Back in London I had dated a conceptual artist. We weren't well suited, but then again who is cut out to make love with the English, really? It's like dealing with a haunted self-catering rental flat behind a pub with a coin-operated heater in Cornwall in the Autumn, near the boulders along the coast where the sea crashes ceaselessly in the rain. When my company was hacked, she exhibited a series of salacious projects drawn from my private emails after a thorough doxxing. She added my face, my name, and my phone number to the series, entitled "INBOX." Then she bought my dark web profile and created a hand-bound "TELEPHONE DIRECTORY OF THE SOUL" based on the results. My hours of price comparisons on hotel packages in Bruges or my repeated inability to learn how to spell the word "Pharaoh" amused many leading critics. My whereabouts looking at owls and miniature deer and eating salted caramel ice cream with my other lover in Clissold Park on Sundays were featured as a series of detailed maps charting my progress through infidelity. She also had recordings of my voice during intimate moments and arguments, "VAMPIRE RADIO," she called it, which seemed to a major critic "artfully ambiguous...who is the host and who is the bloodsucker?" I put in my request to transfer jobs and that is really how I ended up here in Luxembourg. But even now, my minor fame sometimes precedes me. Sometimes there's an "Aren't you that guy...?" giggle at the gallery or the bar. Sometimes the question is a prelude to a form of vitriol. At other times this is the opening gambit in a seduction that gets Instagrammed by my ex.

#

My brother is a real celebrity, a star in a sport that is played only on a semi-pro basis here in Luxembourg. Back home in the States he's face-on-a-display-in-the-supermarket-store famous. He Trends on Twitter and people stop him on the street to request photo opportunities. When I ask him if he would ever like to be completely forgotten by everyone, he says, "Sure, maybe, for a day." *Sic transit gloria,* Soldier, he jokes, quoting an ironic moment in a movie about high school that we often watch together. What really mattered was having a positive impact in other people's lives, he believed. His stationery was embossed with the slogan PURSUING A NATIONAL CHAMPIONSHIP. I was just getting started with morphine. Our stepfather had shouted at me and pushed me around when we were growing up. The guy was a coke addict and didn't know what he was doing sometimes. Then he would become loving and offer to adopt us. My brother was too young to be bullied, or else he exuded a kind of ironclad charisma from the beginning that kept him safe from all harm. Or maybe I had taken the heat off of him without even realizing it at the time. There was some comfort in that thought. I avoided the family home. Really I was only trying to keep my heart afloat by staying late after school, alone, reading pulp fiction about vampires, doppelgangers, dreamworlds, and alternate universes, or listening to the LPs of Alfred Hitchcock introducing macabre short stories on the soft, warm, insulating headphones the local librarian with the sympathetic eyes always had ready for me to connect to the turntable. I couldn't hear a thing other than those outlandishly witty tales of bloodletting and my own breathing. My mother, who was doing her best under the circumstances and soon dumped the guy when she saw clearly where this situation was headed, sent me to a therapist for my insomnia. The therapist gave me a little mantra to repeat to myself before I went to bed: "Today I was a good boy. Today I did fine."

#

As for my mother, she got addicted to a vicious blend of anti-anxiety medication and opioid painkillers after a double hip replacement that was not a success. She told me that *her* mother, my grandmother, who was apparently

undead, visited her at night in a tattered gown and cried out my mother's
name. Her condo, she confided, was falling to pieces and the building would
soon collapse on her as she slept—she showed me tiny cracks in the wall that
"proved" her case. There was something in the water, there was someone she'd
never seen living in a crawlspace or hidden room that was somehow connected to her closet. I stayed with her for a month on a leave of absence, trying to
help out. That's when I started taking morphine. She had an expired prescription in a pint bottle. It was a three-hour struggle to convince her to have a
shower. The water smelt bad and she hated the way it felt on her skin. She
would only eat chicken strips from a sealed envelope and cut green beans mi-
crowaved from a can. A few days after I left in utter despair, taking the bottle
of morphine with me back to Europe, she got on a new antipsychotic drug.
She took the medicine before she went to sleep and never woke up. My brother knew something was wrong and sent firefighters to break down her door,
but it was too late. I still get mail about the class-action suit related to the antipsychotic drug, which had been used heavily in nursing homes and prisons
to sedate unruly patients and prisoners. I use an eyedropper to measure out
the blue-green liquid morphine in my ice-water late at night, staring at my
toes until everything goes deliciously numb and the nightmares begin. Bela
Lugosi had become addicted to morphine and demerol and was buried in his
Dracula costume. My doctor here in Luxembourg is German and she has a
European attitude towards my drug abuse, suggesting that I taper off to a trace
dose over a period of months rather than trying to stop suddenly. You're func-
tional, she says, sighing, I'll write you another maintenance script but try to
avoid needles at all costs. Sometimes we make love under the shared fog of
morphine, or, to tell the truth, she fucks me and then tells me what we're doing is a bad idea. Her bites turn purple, then yellow, with tiny white spots that
reveal the indentations of her little baby devil teeth. Remember me, I plead.
She promises I will never see her again. But then she taps on the window of

the glowing glass of my mobile app, and I invite her back in.

#

When the automatic gate swings shut behind me, late at night outside my flat — shuddering on its metal rails at the touch of a button — sometimes I think I see a dark shape slipping into the parking area. It happens at the corner of my vision, often when I am very tired. I think: What horror have I locked up in here with me? What will it do to get out again?

#

I'm seeing things, so I go to the eye doctor. My eyes are scarred, from the corneal disease I've had for years, and all the damage that's been done to the surface of the corneas from the hard plastic contact lenses that I used to wear. All of our eyes are scarred, he tells me, marked up and traumatized from all the things we've seen. But yours, he adds, are actually scarred. There are scratches where the disease has caused the cornea to break open painfully, oozing a little bit of jelly. This happens every few years. Normally the cornea heals over the scar by itself, but sometimes they have to seal it back up with something like superglue. And what about the dark shapes in the corner, I ask the doctor, the ones that accompany night and morphine? The label says TAKE FOR PAIN, but it doesn't say what kind of pain. The doctor says that the dark shapes are probably the ghosts of cats who have lived in my apartment over the decades, brought in to keep the rats down in the cellars that hold the coffins of the medieval world beneath the streets.

#

I dreamed that I located the missing plane that had been in the news for weeks after it disappeared somewhere over the Pacific. I found myself in a massive airport that reeked of saline. The airport staff were on bicycles, like in Frankfurt, but the location looked tropical outside. I took a wrong turn down a hidden arm of the maze of mall shops selling high-end luggage and electronics accessories. Outside the glass I saw the living dead deplaning on a kind of conveyor belt in a dazed, shuddering, waterlogged mass from an aircraft with unmistakable markings, its wings covered in green mold and its engines choked with seaweed. I started pounding on the glass, and it shattered, bringing a wave of water crashing through the walls of the airport, a flood of handbags and drifting people rushing in like the contents of a shattered aquarium the size of the sky. So that was why the sky was blue! I swam towards the airplane, but it had already started its engines and was rolling away from the airport terminal towards the runways at the sandy bottom of an ocean of brine and sea-trash. I desperately wanted to prove that I had seen the plane, but my phone experienced technical difficulties under the water, snapping only abstract images of shimmering light. I flipped the camera button for a selfie but only more abstract colors emerged from the display. I was a blob of pale lavender trailing what looked like an alarming amount of blood. As the plane revved up and started trundling down a runway for takeoff, it occurred to me that we were at the seafloor and that I had no source of oxygen. The passengers of the missing flight didn't seem to mind, they had some way of breathing the water. They began to arrange the detritus around them into makeshift shelters. As the clouds of my blood gathered around me, so did dark shapes darting into my peripheral vision, fanged sea-snakes, hideous fish with teeth, and then a school of hammerheads whose ancestors had eaten drowned American sailors by the dozen during the Battle of the Coral Sea, and whose descendants had waited in this spot ever since.

#

I wake up in the middle of the night to a soothing Irish voice from the BBC World Service describing the death of my old friend from high school. We had survived a fling, became confidants, and had kept our vow to exchange letters every month for life. She had lived as an adventure journalist—her letters had postmarks that inspired jealousy. I'm motorcycling through Pakistan, her cards would say, or Here's the truth about Transylvania. When she passed through Frankfurt I would drive from Luxembourg City to her airport hotel for the night. I've absorbed so many people, she told me once as we cuddled in a Marriott Courtyard near Mainz, their faces have passed into mine, can you see them? That old idea about photographs and souls was partly right, she had concluded, the picture didn't steal your soul exactly but it multiplied you and made you undead. She died of heat stroke while on assignment in Uganda while tracing the source of the Nile with a film crew for a documentary team that planned to follow the river from its headwaters to Alexandria, and through each successive stage of human culture, from the time before the Pharaohs to present-day political turmoil. This crescendo of fake profundity had acquired worldwide distribution after the tragedy involving my friend. The person with the soothing voice describes how my friend perished in a dry swamp, among strangers who could not help her find ice or water to cool her body, thousands of miles away from her home ground. The medical problem, the program revealed, was that my friend had traveled in the winter from New York City, where it was below freezing, to ninety-degree mornings unprotected by shade. This swing in temperatures had killed her, making hydration impossible and shutting down her body under the direct heat of the sun. Now that the documentary had been released, the filmmakers were on tour, and my beautiful friend's death formed a valuable highlight for their media appearances.

#

Then I lose my job, after weeks of habitual lateness and morphine nodouts at my dual-screen terminal overlooking the Athens stock market. I miss the moment just before the dead-cat bounce when our strategy required a massive cash infusion to the National Bank of Greece at the very instant its shares hit bottom. We were supposed to load in and then withdraw during the first split second of after-hours trading. Our clients were supposed to feast on the financial chaos and then siphon off their fair share of the latest money transfusion, a quick pinch of the blood-bag. Three minutes late, and I'm buying inflated shares that lose half their value the very next day after another twist in the epic poem of Greek financial markets involving a rumor about the secret printing of drachmas in advance of a potential expulsion from the single currency. My total losses on a single trade: A company record 75 million Euros. The clients need an offering, my supervisor tells me. I am to be executed via web conference with a jewel-encrusted blade, the contents of my heart shared out among the ancient toasting bowls of the board of directors. Looking for work elsewhere, I bring my empty briefcase to the headhunters. Somebody has put me on the blacklist, they tell me, in this business when you're dead you stay dead, pointing at my gaping chest, where my silk tie fails to disguise the void in my ribcage. I'm still very wealthy from all my years helping to manage the destruction of humanity. The doctor who supplies my morphine in exchange for sex prescribes another bottle of liquid evil and suggests a vacation at her family's ruined ancestral castle in the wine country near Colmar. I am convinced that if I go away with her I will never be seen alive again. Instead I stuff my briefcase with contact lens solution, deodorant, and underwear, then board a train headed East.

#

I am writing from the city of Trier, ancient home of Holy Roman Emperors, where I float in a river of morphine and dry Mosel Riesling, henna hair dye and spa resorts amidst the distillation of catastrophic history from the time before Constantine to the aftermath of Hitler. Even though you are dead I cannot help writing to you anyway, my dear old friend with the lovely neck. I hold out hope that you might be able to hear me, still, somehow, on a secret wavelength. Please know that I would gladly feed you my own fatty liver if it meant you might return from the grave even for an evening.

My grandfather was stationed in Trier after the war, in a displaced persons camp that the United Nations established on the cliffs above the city in

1945. He never talked about what happened in the camp, so I have always imagined the worst. Russian POWs on death marches from the sub-camps and slave quarries of the Rhineland gathered in Trier, afraid to return home after the war because they had been branded traitors by Stalin merely for having survived the Nazis. The camp overlooked Roman ruins and the artillery-shattered modern city. Non-fraternization rules prohibited contact with the locals, so they marched four miles, down the hills and around the city walls, just to have a bath. In France and Belgium, things had been different. Ladies of the town welcomed American GIs (or at least their money) in Pont-a-Mousson, and Marlene Dietrich had performed for the troops in Nancy in '44.

A few days ago, when I was wandering down the hill in an effort to re-trace my grandfather's footsteps, I saw a man with my father's face, in a brown cardigan, waiting for a city bus at a shelter outside a superstore on the outskirts. The closer I looked, the more similar to my father the man appeared, and I could not help accosting him. He did not know what I wanted, and my pointing gestures and broken German probably made me appear like a madman.

I pointed at his face, then pointed at my face, then pointed at his face. You... I stammered... You are me?

He spat and gathered his things to leave, crossing the pleasant clean bridge that was constructed from the red stone that had doomed so many political prisoners from across Europe to the Nazi quarries. I followed him until it became clear that he was terrified.

We crossed paths again yesterday in the crypt of the great Cathedral in the old city, standing within a few feet of one another near the reliquary that holds the skull of Saint Helena. She had brought fragments of the True Cross back to Europe from the Middle East and gave birth to Constantine, the Emperor who made the West a Christian land. The reliquary was closed, but the man assured me that I was in the right place, and asked me, in what sounded like Eastern European-inflected English, why I had chased him at the bus stop.

You look like my father, I said. Trier plays tricks on the mind, he said. Is it really her skull inside there? I asked. The English say she was English royalty, he said, but maybe she was a stable-maid from Turkey. The marriage might have taken place in Serbia, he added, or perhaps Constantine was a love-child, do I have this phrase correct? She was buried in Rome and yet her skull winds up in Trier, like yours and mine. I was born here in a refugee camp up on the hill, he said, but we couldn't stay here, we had to go back to Budapest, I found my way back after Schengen.

Your father was an American? I asked him, my heart leaping with fear.

No, he said, tears springing to his eyes.

His story was much worse than that.

#

Somebody has been writing in my notebook while I am out walking around the city. I return to my hotel only to find new notes, descriptions of my worst memories, and little fragments giving glimpses into the inner workings of a disturbed mind. It's all in my own scrawl. This bothers me less than the fact that some of the most intimate tidbits have started appearing online, as a series of confessions published under my name. I read an announcement of an upcoming literary event in which I am scheduled to appear, and I wonder if this is another one of my ex's practical jokes. She's become an installation artist, and maybe this is a new project in which she will hire an actor to pretend to be me. A celebrity profile emerges in a respected glossy magazine complete with excerpts from a searing autobiography soon to be published. I wonder what I will have to say about myself.

#

At first I thought the person following me around the city might be a stalker or perhaps—a more cheerful thought—a surveillance tail sent by some agency that had deemed me a person of sufficient interest to bother bothering. But the man turns out to be nothing more than a bureaucrat from the Dept. of Art, he claims, sent to make sure I am spending my days wisely. He approaches me while I am sitting on the grassy steps of the Roman amphitheater just outside of town.

People crave entertainment, he tells me, you must respect yourself enough as an artist to become involved with the issues of the day. Put some elbow grease into it, he continues, try to write something more substantial than all these little disconnected thoughts you jot down in your notebook.

Is that an order? I ask.

Give us a character we can root for, he pleads, for heaven's sake, would it kill you to write what people want to read? What about a historical novel? Something with some research in it. Or maybe something autobiographical, about your family roots, something along those lines?

How do you know about that? I ask.

From scanning your email, he says, we take an interest in art here.

You don't really work for the government, do you? I ask. You really don't know anything about me.

That's just the problem! he says, shaking his head. Now, he said, read what you've just written.

*A specter is haunting Europe,* I read from the page.

Pretentious twaddle! he says, but gestures for me to continue.

*It's not really true that blondes have more fun,* I read. *Sometimes blondes have significantly less fun. All unhappy families are the same...a thing of joy is a beauty forever...*

Rubbish! he says.

I'm afraid I have nothing to say, I say.

Who did that ever stop before? Tap into your soul!

How?

Try this, he says, handing me a little packet of white powder.

Oh, I get it now, you're a salesman!

Fifty Euro, he says, suddenly solemn.

The stuff he sells me is unbelievably good, but when you feel good there really is no reason in the world to write anything.

#

I see an English-language sign advertising VAMPIRE LOVERS down near the river, in the mini-Red Light District by the Karl Marx House Museum. I have to call the number, just to find out what will happen next. A towering blonde person with a thin face and exhausted lavender eyes arrives at my hotel room. With their wildflower tiara and black velvet cape they look like they had just stepped out of some medieval woods in a paranormal romance eBook.

My people are from the forests, they say.

Okay, I say, so how does this work?

Do you know what ethics are? they ask, drawing out a scalpel and carving a tiny "X" on my chest at the solar plexus, where the wings of my rib cage start to diverge.

Ethics, I say, as they lap at a small pool of my blood.

Reciprocity, they say, or even altruism, if such a remarkable thing indeed might be said to exist.

*A specter is haunting Europe*, I say.

I taste loads of Riesling and something else that's not too nice, they say.

Morphine. Want some?

They take the bottle, hold it up to the light, and frown. Then they pour the contents out on the carpet, very quickly, before I can do anything about it. I leap to the floor and kneel to suck some of the liquid out of the artificial fibers. When I resurface, the ethical vampire is clucking at me in disappointment. Very matter of fact, very German. I'm horrified when I see what they see, in the mirror, the drug smeared over my mouth along with carpet-threads and dust.

You have to stop before it becomes about the needle, they say. Most fatalities occur as a result of the improper use of hypodermics.

Your English is excellent, I say.

They wince and burp, clearly tasting something... unclean.

As agreed in advance, they hold my hand for what seems like hours while I shiver and scream and weep. It feels like some evil presence is gradually withdrawing from my body, a kind of dark liquid that emanates from my mouth and ears, transforms into mist, gathers into a small cloud, and then winds its way through the window glass, pausing as if to say a fond goodbye.

When I wake up before sunrise, the tall person is gone and I have a bandage carefully affixed to my heart. I'm itching everywhere, and feel an irresistible urge to pace. I walk down to the river with my briefcase, rent a bicycle, and start riding South-West out of Trier as fast as I can, trying to deal with my restless legs by gliding along the river in a blind sprint. Moving seems to help.

This was the same route my grandfather's military unit took from France to Germany during the war, only I am reversing the direction, and, therefore, going backwards in time. It's not long before dead American GIs appear, floating face-down in the river where the vineyards converge on the banks of the Mosel, ruined towns smoldering above me, supply convoys and light artillery evaporating as I pass through the lines of reinforcements pushing deeper into Germany.

It's only three hours to the French border, with views of liberated Luxembourgish farmers waving greetings and bottles much of the way. After sunset I finally arrive in Metz, which has been heavily shelled, and settle into a seedy room with peeling wallpaper, rats in the walls, and massive water damage from broken plumbing. For several days, I cannot eat anything without puking, but then, as the physical symptoms of my addiction recede, I begin thinking about the vampire person in Trier, who must have been a figment of my imagination, like the man with my father's face in the Cathedral and all the rest of my recent hallucinations and flimsy dreams. No good witch waits in the forest with a cure, the True Cross sold to Saint Helena was a nothing more than a bundle of crooked timber, no final triumph exists around the next bend in the river of time, and a decade of Nazi radio broadcasts are even now expanding into deep space, they will outpace us to the ears of intelligent life on other planets.

We all have so much explaining to do.

#

My brain cooks itself, as with a flame under a spoon, in an attempt to keep me alive. I am not certain whether I am awake or dreaming, but it seems that I have been deported, although I have no memory of having traveled.

I see a different city outside my hotel room window. It's a dusty and colorful place filled with evening bats, graffiti-choked walls of glorious intricacy, and the smell of incense rising from the little square near an old church.

The streets are deserted but the church doors are open. The chapel is empty and the altar is encased in massive quantities of gold. Presumably this is Spain and I'm looking at loot from the New World. I pray for an end to the feeling that my face is warping and expanding under its fever. I pass out and come to under the solicitous fingers of a janitor, but I cannot understand his words of comfort and stumble outside, where a crowd has gathered to listen to a mournful brass band serenading the Virgin and the moon and the lottery kiosk with the lucky black cats painted into the tile.

Romans used to rule here, and then the Caliphate, and then the Inquisition, and then the Fascists, and now the lottery.

What place is this? I ask a passerby who looks like a fellow tourist, a man in white socks and a t-shirt that reads THE WALKING DEAD.

We're at the periphery of the Eurozone, he says with a smirk.

You have to help me, I say.

Do I? he says.

I'm an American, I say.

Then use your credit card, he says.

He starts to walk away, and I lose him in the crowds milling around the brass band. The tiny streets wind into medieval lanes, which branch into plazas of silent apartment blocks FOR SALE OR RENT, secret banyans and entrances to hidden chapels.

I encounter a group of men practicing lifting up the great statue of the Virgin, with their shirts slung into makeshift headdresses, a stack of concrete blocks standing in for the massive weight of the statue they will be carrying in an upcoming religious procession.

When they notice me watching them, they start to murmur and then to hiss. I can't tell what has upset them, whether it's that I have interrupted their ritual or whether it's some other impropriety related to my way of dressing or my atrocious manners or simply my existence.

A delegation comes over to explain something about *"tarde,"* and it dawns on me that they think I am someone else, a member of the group who has arrived late for this important gathering.

*Soy de America*, I explain, *lo siento.*

That idea makes them laugh and clap one another on the back, shaking their heads at my antics, waiting for me to stop joking around, return to being the person they think they are addressing, and merge back into the group.

*Yo estoy muy enfermo*, I add.

The penitents look me up and down carefully. Then one of them shows me a knife, flashing it in front of me as if he is dealing with a person who might be possessed. He beckons towards me with the knife, but I decline his invitation, hobbling away on rubber legs, hoping that he decides I am not worth chasing down. The relevant folklore is universal. If he stabs me in a certain spot and I do not bleed in a satisfactory fashion, that will mean the end of me.

#

I awake to find my window overlooking a Martian desert. We have been sent here in the false belief that the ice-caps of the Red Planet could be mined for water, but there's something toxic in polar zones. The ochre surface of the planet does not derive from the rust of infinite cities, there's nothing here. But when I speak of boredom, you cannot possibly imagine the scale of it. I keep asking for permission to return home, sending communiques outlining my belief that I should be replaced by a robot, since a manned mission is nothing more than an expensive vanity project at this stage. One day, after failing to hear from Earth for several weeks, I decide to walk out into the desert without my oxygen helmet and look for a place to die. That's when I discover, to my confusion and shock, that I am able to breathe in the atmosphere without any significant problems. Everything clicks into place, and I jab a screwdriver into my forearm to take a look at my wiring. The radio transmitter broadcasts news from Earth about the diminishing oceans. I finally recognize what I am, a self-repairing immortal who can feed from solar energy and continue to exist as long as I have spare parts, which will sustain me for centuries in this dry environment. I will make it my life's ambition to try to forget or delete all the false memories of green places and family gatherings that have been implanted in my whirring mechanical brain. I can tear out my eyes and then set them in place again. They gave me something like the equivalent of tinnitus which I have been unable to fix so far. I am the only thinking thing on this planet and there must have been a deliberate decision made not to deliver me home in the event that my mission proved useless. Instead, they abandoned me. From what I can gather about humans, I wouldn't be surprised if they started drinking each other's blood when they ran out of water. One idea kept me going, an implanted memory from a family vacation to Costa Rica, far away from the reach of armies and filled with water. Maybe this was the restart point, maybe someday someone would remember what had happened and come looking for me. It wasn't plausible but the idea still brought me comfort.

#

This time the doors of my hotel window open on a desert city of glass skyscrapers, somewhere out in the dried-up and now lawless part of the country. Heavily-armed security guards patrol the plazas between the towers, which stand empty, whistling in the sand. At one time these properties were considered investments too valuable to spoil or damage by actually inhabiting them. The city gradually became like a vast treasure chest, with each building like a bar of gold. Then one day everyone realized that the buildings were not gold, of course, but merely glass, and that the city was just a colossal construction site. The whole place crumbled to ruins without anybody really noticing what had happened, since the losses could be interpreted as tax write-offs. Refugees from conflict zones moved in for a time. These squatters established a new city-state, neutral in all wars, a zone in which all were welcome to sleep amidst the illimitable failed real estate ventures. Without an army, they were quickly swept away into makeshift towns near the river when the government restored order with the national guard. A mogul had purchased the entire city for pennies on the dollar, with the intent to redevelop the downtown into the world's largest casino, convention center, and sex-positive entrepreneurial zone. After the street battles were over, the billionaire sent in the security guards while negotiating the financing with an international group of sovereign wealth funds, more proof of the fundamentally optimistic nature of humankind. Lithium and a secret ingredient, said to be a mixture of biological immortals such as sea urchins, certain jellyfish, sanicula herbs, endangered New Zealand black coral, and mother's milk, would be pumped into the water supply, which traveled hundreds of miles from the snowpack of the Rockies through an elaborate system of aqueducts. I must be a kind of land-surveyor, or part of a location-scouting crew for a promo film, or perhaps some sort of advertising pamphlet-writer, sent out in advance to live rent-free in exchange for glowing reports that can be used to lure in new capital from ordinary investors in Asia seeking a stake in the American Dream. Drone footage displays the view from their window and provides virtual tours of the property. I have been made to feel that my life depends on a positive report, but my last few attempts to sell my soul have been returned with curt comments: "I didn't fall in love," "Lacks realism," "Overly negative," and "Tell us a story we can really sink our teeth into."

#

Another thing that didn't happen, now in the past tense. If I remember rightly, my company in Luxembourg once sent me to report on an entire city, which had gone bankrupt, as a potential takeover prospect by a consortium of activist hedge funds masquerading as dark web hackers, known informally as Les Vampires. Everyone knew my reputation for bending the truth. This city was unusual insofar as it contained nothing except a gigantic Cathedral, so large that it could only be viewed in its entirety from outer space. Its chapels were neighborhoods and its altars were mansion houses and its tombs were expansive enough to shelter entire families. Inside a chapel you'd find a painting with a scene that contained a chapel with a painting, and eventually you saw that you were living inside the painting, or rather that your whole life took place inside a corner of the painting. A string of copywriters had been dispatched before me into the city, never to return. Tourist images revealed that they had been glazed into mosaics, as a kind of frieze representing the folly of greed. The tourists themselves had been immolated later on in a fired-clay allegory of voyeurism voyeurized, a cruel and pedantic misstep on the part of the Cathedral authorities that reeked of the medieval mindset of Dante, if you ask me. But I volunteered for this land-surveying job cheerfully, confident that at least I would wind up serving some larger purpose than myself, sacrificing my life to contribute a small tile in some larger picture that might delight or unsettle some future visitor to the Cathedral city.

#

Where was I? I'll continue in past tense since this is a letter about things that never happened. When I reached the gates of the great Cathedral, whose famous tower had once held a muezzin and whose chapel held the bones of the man who first brought Europeans to the New World, I was accosted by a pitiful sweating man with excellent English who swore he could grant me access to a secret tour.

When one rejects God, it is much worse than not knowing Him at all. This is, in truth, a terrible crime, like slapping a child in the face when the child has opened its hand to comfort you. Death awaits, then Hell, you cannot pretend that you didn't know the rules. That's why I found the Cathedral so unsettling. Its haul of artifacts, relics, sacred fingerbones, Old Masters, towering walls of gold, and the world's second-largest pearl failed to move me. I was dead inside, a lost soul grazing on food meant to sustain faith in the inexplicable mystery of the existence of the universe, exchanging lustful glances with damned faces drawn to this spot from all over Europe.

My family, the man confided in a whisper as he led me into a dark alcove, preferred to worship at this altar, and now you'll see why.

We were looking at a famous statue of a child with pursed lips who closed his eyes perpetually in the gloom behind glass, while pilgrims left flowers and sprigs as offerings at his tiny bare feet.

After my mother died, the man continued, audible but barely visible, I came to church less frequently. My father, he said, refused to go at all, without her it was too painful to absorb Christ's lies about our inevitable reunion in the afterlife. When I did return to this altar, he said, pointing at something above the statue that I couldn't make out, I noticed something very strange. In the niche above the altar, he said, pointing, I saw this smoke-darkened painting.

He inched closer to the statue and pointed insistently. I saw the canvas he was talking about, but I couldn't discern that it had anything on it except soot.

You see for yourself, he said, that it is a painting of the blackness of darkness forever.

It could use a cleaning, I said.

Look closer and you'll notice something odd about it, he said.

I blinked and peered, and as my contact lenses adjusted to the low light in the cool air, I heard the sound of the bells from the modern trams passing outside, filtered through the massive ancient doors. The doors made an unnerving whistling sound in the wind, slamming shut with great force unless the visitors knew to close them gently.

I see a figure, I said.

The painting above the altar did have a subject after all. The figure appeared to be stooped unnaturally, as if deformed or broken-backed. And the figure seemed to have horns, or something sharp and curved protruding from a deeper darkness like an anti-halo around its head.

You see it, he said, good, I used to stand here for hours and stare at the painting. If you wait long enough, you might see a pair of foul eyes.

It's not a member of the Holy Family, I said.

Was it the child below the painting that we were worshiping all those years, he asked, rhetorically, or was it this thing in the painting? One day I gathered the courage to ask the deacon.

What happened? I asked.

This was a man who had witnessed my baptism, he said, in the ancient stone basin under the eyes of the wooden saints.

You don't need to lard it on, I said.

So I asked him, the man said, what is that, the creature in the painting above the little statue of the baby Jesus that pilgrims travel to visit from all over the world?

Again, I said, you are trying too hard now, do you want a tip or not at the end of this story?

At first, the man continued, ignoring me, the deacon pretended not to know what I was talking about...or about which I was talking?

Go ahead, I said.

Which is the correct English usage?

It doesn't matter, I said.

No, but I would like to learn better English, he said.

English is a language you speak less well the more you use it, I said.

Sorry?

You had it right. The English idiom would be "what I was talking about."

But that's not correct.

That's correct, I said.

It's correct that it's not correct?

It's correct that it's correct that it's not correct. You could *write* "about which I was talking" but you would *say* "what I was talking about."

In God's name, why? This is a corrupted language, no? I mean, look at the Anglosphere now. You really flushed yourselves down the drain.

Please go on with your story.

The deacon looked alarmed, the man continued, his eyes twinkling, so I knew I was on to something. "On to something"?

Yes, I said, go on.

I pressed the deacon, he said, and finally he admitted that there was more to the story. Nobody has asked about this dark painting in years, he tells me, it's an image we are instructed never to discuss. Why not? Because, the deacon tells me, nobody really knows what this picture is. Who painted it? We don't know. When was it placed inside the Church? We don't know. There are no records of it ever having been commissioned.

How can that be? I asked.

The deacon tells me, the man continued, this is a painting that nobody wants to have cleaned. Nobody wants to know what the image underneath looks like. There is a rumor that the painting is Roman, or pre-Roman. There is a belief among the local clergy and some archaeologists that another place of worship has always existed here. The Romans and the Kings and the Caliphs and the Church and the modern State have built their cities on the spot of a tomb where something evil waits forever to be set free to feed on the hearts and souls of men.

This final Spanish flourish was too much for me, over elaborate and strained. I walked off in a huff into another chapel, knowing that I had been duped by this fake local guide seeking English grammar lessons. I thought about all the superstitious vibes controlling the city, the way that people moved from lifting the saints in the holiday processions during the day to calling the tarot readers and phone sex lines and lottery shows on television at night. My guide did not pursue me in the hopes of being paid, either he knew he had failed to persuade me or he was severely mentally ill.

I exited the Cathedral, taking a path away from the cursed painting, and headed out into the sunshine, crossing the bridge into Triana to look at tile shops. As I glanced down into the river water, I distinctly heard a whispering voice asking mildly in elegant Spanish if anyone would mind if I jumped. Crowds of tourists passed, mostly Americans in jeans and white socks wearing college logo t-shirts and families wielding selfie sticks. None of these people had spoken to me, and for a moment I was truly convinced that the evil painting had affixed itself to me. Then I saw the man from the Cathedral nodding at me from a distance of a few yards, too far away, I thought, to have said something that sounded like a whisper in my ear. I paid him twenty Euros, and he thanked me profusely without ever moving his lips. I would be lying if I told you that was the last time I heard his voice.

#

I'm back at home in the States now—if you can call it "home" when it feels like a foreign country possessed by demons—having survived a near-miss with the authorities in Luxembourg on my way out of Europe. I have a wedding band but I don't remember any ceremony. I have disordered souvenirs from countries I can barely recall passing through, postcards and pamphlets for palaces and airports I do not remember visiting. Have I collected mementos of all the things I failed to see? Strange liqueurs from across the Eurozone keep arriving by mail, bottles of blood-red sugary liquid scented with cherries and roses, postmarked from Trier. While I was away, someone rummaged through my bank account. The money's been restored by the fraud division, but I continue to receive threatening calls demanding wire transfers to Romania. Some of the calls feature very realistic screaming in the background, phony staged hostage situations featuring relatives I don't have, and I make certain to applaud the spirit of entrepreneurship. If only I had had more courage to reply with an invitation when the lovely German concierge at the airport hotel had smiled and said, "One room, one person, one night?" But no, she was only doing her job, and it was silly of me not to know the difference at this point in my life. Anyway it appeared that I was married, to whom or where or why, I couldn't say. If only there really were someone out there, a figure in a dark cape with black lipstick beckoning at my window to join her out in the fog.

#

Just trying to gather my notes and thoughts together from my imaginary journeys, so that I can make another little hand-sewn book of letters never sent to you, my dear, departed friend, like we did in high school. You were always the friend of my mind, you were the closest thing I ever had to a home. What is it the man says in *Dracula,* about how a friend is rarer than a lover? I still can't help wondering whether you have some way of listening, beyond death, on a frequency that isn't yet known to science.

My biggest regret about leaving morphine behind is that I cannot visit you anymore, your voice has vanished, I don't remember my dreams. I can't tune in. I am getting healthier and physically fit, the cranberry juice detox and organic raspberry binges have cleared up the blockages around my heart, my doctor is talking about a garlic liver miracle, and I feel totally undead inside, like I am floating face down in my life.

I watch my brother on television, he's now coaching the national Olympic team, clapping his hands and encouraging the youth stars of tomorrow to rebound. He sends me texts with inspirational quotations from Thomas DeQuincey's *Suspiria de profundis* that help me make it through the night.

The horror of life without morphine is that nothing sticks, everything tastes like ashes, and a weight like a backpack filled with bricks grows heavy on my spine. I go to the movies, and even the vampires are trying their best to be nice to everybody, their need to fit in makes me sad, and in these new movies nobody falls into a room of barbed wire.

I buy a set of plastic teeth to wear on the train, giving certain passengers a smiling glimpse of an alternative to an ordinary commute. The lost or unwritten works of DeQuincey haunt me, with their opium-laced hints of "Foundering Ships," "Faces! Angels' Faces!," and "The Dreadful Infant."

My brother invites me to tag along on a goodwill tour of Iran, where basketball fever is strong—but so is heroin, and I'm afraid that if I leave home I will end up relapsing and embarrassing everyone. Our Lady of Tears, Our Lady of Sighs, and Our Lady of Darkness no longer pay their respects from the shadows in the corners of rooms and darkened streets and staircases.

Besides my brother, the person I admire most in the world is Louise Brooks, the silent movie star who, later in life, divorced her millionaire husband, went bankrupt, worked as a call-girl and a shop girl, got hooked on sleeping pills and lost in gin, wrote a book about her life and then burned it.

I'm writing to you from my hotel in snowy Rochester, where I visited the graves of Brooks and Francis Tumblety, the fake doctor whose handwriting most closely resembles that of Jack the Ripper. He had lived in Whitechapel during the murders in 1888. He fled London after attracting the attention of the police. You may have heard of him—he's the Ripper suspect who displayed a collection of specimen jars in his study...

At the end of Pabst's 1929 film *Pandora's Box*, Brooks, the immortal vamp who is forevermore in fashion, finds herself broke on Christmas Eve in London, and winds up exchanging her body for a warm place to stay. The man fate chooses for her is the infamous serial killer of Whitechapel. But when it was released in France the ending of this film was changed—Brooks is declared innocent and joins the Salvation Army instead. Maybe Tumblety disapproved of this cut to his screen time and found some extra-dimensional magnetism to draw Brooks to him on the shores of Lake Ontario during her final years? But no, Brooks would have defeated him through her own alchemy. Hers is the face that will remain forever unaltered.

I have imagined a third, lost ending to the film, in which Brooks laughs at being stabbed and sinks her fangs into the killer, explaining that she is older than Nefertiti and that she will never die because her entire body is cast from silver nitrate, liable to explosions and deathless unquenchable fire. The burning bush was a time-traveler with an old decaying flammable can of film. Everybody knows that.

The figure at the cemetery dressed all in black... No, I'm lying again, it's the dead of winter here and I was entirely alone in the deep snow, shivering with my bundle of roses in front of Brooks' grave, pressing the thorns into my fingers through my thin cheap fleece gloves. The voice that seemed to emanate from beneath the snow...nobody will believe that even though it's true. Brooks had a wonderful voice, but she never had much luck with sound pictures.

#

I still daydream about where I might have been, where I was, and where

I am now. On my last day in Europe, I drove back into Luxembourg City from Metz to retrieve some personal effects from my flat and to visit my doctor to see if she would give me some morphine for my journey home. The GPS software was outdated and flashed a warning on the display—DANGEROUS: THIS ROUTE PASSES THROUGH LUXEMBOURG. Luxembourg is not a country I associate with danger, but I suppose in my case the comment was accurate enough, given my purpose there. I had passed through physical withdrawal, so my urge to relapse was purely perverse, a last-ditch attempt to destroy myself.

My doctor was not answering her mobile phone, so I drove to her office and tried to wheedle a prescription renewal out of one of her colleagues, a compassionate-looking older Frenchman in a cardigan and owlish glasses that he placed on a springy cord around his neck. Something about the man made me want to confess everything, but as soon as I reached the airport I was sorry I had done so. The man looked physically sick by the end of my story.

The Luxembourgish detectives did not seem to think they were as funny as I did. In their gloves and plainclothes suits they looked to me like identical twins working as very high-toned butlers. They spoke to each other in Luxembourgish and to me in impeccable boarding-school-in-Britain English. They had received an anonymous tip that I might be attempting to smuggle drugs across international borders, and in any event my visa had been canceled when I had left my job.

I guess you'll have to deport me, I said, which is convenient because my flight is scheduled to depart in three hours.

They had been through my luggage and discovered my notebook, which was clogged with bizarre anecdotes of drug abuse and insulting commentary about their country. Before they let me go they wanted to know the identity of the doctor who had supplied me with morphine illegally.

It's all fiction, I said, isn't that obvious by now?

It says here in your notebook, a detective said, that the royal family of Luxembourg are vampires.

But you know who the real vampires are, the other detective said.

*A specter is haunting Europe,* I said.

What does this mean? the first detective said.

It's druggie gibberish, the second detective said.

*Nosferatu,* I whispered.

They left me to mull things over until I had missed my flight. A representative of the American consulate—a blonde jock named Dale on a junior-year internship abroad—dropped by with a printout of lawyers' contact numbers and canned remarks about obeying local laws and noninterference in the legitimate process of justice.

Dale, are you at Yale? I asked the kid.

Princeton, he said, shrugging, everyone needs a safety school.

Don't go into the financial services industry after college. Look where it got me.

Don't worry, the kid said, I'm working on an app.

I sighed.

Okay, I said. Go ahead. What's the pitch for your app?

So, Dale said, when you install the app, it automatically adds .1% of every purchase you make on your phone to a carefully vetted charity of your choice. Homeless veterans, clean water, minority scholarships, malaria vaccinations, planting trees, and so on.

Can I invest in your company? I said.

No, he said, there's no company, no profit, no overhead, no administrative costs. I don't take any salary. The money is diverted electronically from every transaction. It adds up over time into billions.

It's like a tip you add to the bill, I said. A tip for... you know...

Precisely.

What's the app called?

RobbinHoodie.

I sighed again, but the idea seemed viable.

Who are the fiduciaries?

People in banking, he said, but, not, like, disgraced drug addicts, sorry. Well, it was nice chatting, good luck with your, uh, legal jeopardy situation and stuff.

After another hour passed, someone new dropped by, a wonderfully plump middle aged henna-haired mysterian in a pantsuit and cape with laughing eyes and twisted teeth. She pushed a small bottle of codeine across the table.

We can offer you a deal, she said.

*Unclean, unclean,* I muttered.

You'll report to us, she said.

To who?

Whom, she said, correcting my English grammar.

The last vestige of the dative was fading.

To whom? I said.

You'll be our man in Washington, she said.

D.C.?

You'll submit a monthly report to our embassy, she said.

On what?

Varied topics connected with economic dealings.

What for?

Industrial espionage related to the banking sector.

I'm unemployable.

We'll recommend you for a certain job. We'll find you a good doctor to help you.

To help me get off drugs or to keep me on them?

Whichever makes you more productive in the burgeoning field of industrial espionage.

You want me to betray my country?

No, just certain companies.

*A specter is haunting Europe.*

Yes. No. You'll draw a comfortable salary. An apartment in the suburbs. The quiet life.

What are your aims? I asked.

To compete in today's increasingly globalized marketplace.

But more specifically…?

You'll supply personal details on your colleagues. Especially those who travel frequently to Europe. If they have preferences or weaknesses. This sort of information. Leverage worth money. Details we might exchange with other countries, depending on whether it suits our interests. At key moments in delicate negotiations.

So you want me to screw over douchebag financiers, I said.

Think of yourself as a vampire hunter, she said.

Luxembourg has spies? I said. Come on.

A few.

In the States?

Who can say?

How can you trust me? I said.

Either you'll get results or we'll, you know.

Have me killed?

This is Luxembourg! We're not going to slip polonium into your tea.

I want…

Yes?

I want a gorgeous and flirtatious secret contact who meets with me in mysterious settings all over the city. We will grow affectionate over the years but the timing will never be right to act on our passionate impulses.

It's going to be less glamorous than that. A numbers station. Do you know what that is?

No.

It's a radio transmission with a string of numbers. Our station is called Vampire Radio. We'll supply you with a codebook that tells you what the numbers mean. You'll pose as an amateur ham radio enthusiast. No email. No phone contact. You'll buy a used typewriter for your reports. You'll hand deliver your reports to a dead drop located in the embassy during hours when the building is open for cultural events.

This is getting very specific very quickly, I said.

This is a job offer, she said, and you won't see me again.

*J'accepte.*

#

Maybe the Grand Duchy of Luxembourg pays me to write these fictions, in the hopes of creating a false impression of their global reach and international influence. Anything's possible with that kind of money. They pay me to spy on my own country. I won't apologize for trying my best to observe what I see, even if it is not there. I'm like the festive short man I saw riding the Metro today in the direction of the National Mall. He had a plastic bag filled with soft fabric rags. He went around the train car with his rags. Whenever he found an empty seat, he carefully wiped it down. He took his time and savored his work, stooping to clean the seats, running the rag over the silver handrails, and even polishing the seat-backs of the next row. Then, when new passengers boarded the train, he sat back and furtively watched them sitting in the seats he had so assiduously cleaned. He lurked, smiling slightly, in an ebullient mood, admiring his handiwork. I didn't let on that I saw what he was doing, because I thought that he preferred to work in secret, unpaid. Surely this was not a hobby as much as a compulsion. If this man was any different from me, I think it was only in ways that reflected well on him.

#

A strange thing happened to me recently. Walking alone in the woods, near dark, at the spot in the vast National Park where a Congressional intern had notoriously met her end, I was meditating on my sins. It dawned on me that I hadn't had a live conversation with another real human being—face to face, not screen to screen—in days. A very tall jogger in a hoodie—splendid violet eyes, doubly masked up in black and gray—passed by, adjusting their earphones. Something about this person made me turn around. When I looked back, I saw that they had stopped as well, and turned around to look at me. It was the ethical vampire from Trier, or a person who looked very much like them. No, it wasn't them, after all. It was their doppelganger, and not so ethical. Everything got very still and the light seemed to die on the leaves around me. The person had a too-thin face, almost two-dimensional, and a very, very thin body that looked wasted from horrible torturous exercise. A hand reached for an ear and plucked one of the sports earphones out. Then the person started jogging in place and singing the words of a song I had never heard before, and never want to hear again. *Don't worry,* went the refrain, *you've only got a few years left.*

## Contributors

**Joseph Alcala** is a writer from Indiana. He writes the Substack blog the thought of the thing and was formerly a managing editor of genesis *Literary & Art Magazine*. He is at work on several pieces of fiction and nonfiction.

**Rachel Coyne** is a writer and painter from Lindstrom, MN.

**Mathew Gostelow** (he/him) is a dad, husband, and author, living in Birmingham, UK. Some days he wakes early and writes strange tales. If you catch him staring into space, he is either thinking about Twin Peaks or cooked breakfasts. He has published two collections: a book of speculative short stories called *See My Breath Dance Ghostly* (*Alien Buddha Press*) and *Connections*, a flash fiction chapbook (*Naked Cat Publishing*). Mat was nominated for the *Pushcart Prize* in 2022 and *Best of the Net* in 2023. You can find him on Twitter: @MatGost.

**Bronwen Harding** is a writer from Liverpool, UK, with an MA in English Literature. She's had poetry published by *Word Vomit Zine*, *Ram Eye Press*, and *Bent Key Press*, and is currently a poetry editor for *Thin Veil Press*. She grew up watching horror films with her dad, and then coming up with post-structuralist ecocritical feminist analyses of them over cups of tea. Her Twitter/X handle is @BronwenHarding.

**Carolin Jesussek** is a German PhD candidate and writer of short stories and poetry. She's currently working on her dissertation about contemporary gothic literature.

**Janice Leadingham** is a Portland, OR based writer and tarot reader originally from somewhere-near-Dollywood, Tennessee. You can find her work in *HAD*, *The Bureau Dispatch*, *Reckon Review*, *the Northwest Review*, and *Bullshit Lit*, among others. She is @TheHagSoup on Twitter and Instagram, and hagsoup.com.

**Sarah Lofgren** creates B2B copy by day and speculative nonsense at night. She's a writer, choreographer, and illustrator living in Seattle. Her favorite animals are sea otters and her short stories have appeared in publications including *Human Parts* and *Jane Austen's Wastebasket*. For more info visit sarahlofgren.com.

*Flexible Press* published **Bob McNeil**'s book composed of essays, illustrations, poems, and stories titled *Compositions on Compassion and Other Emotions*. A portion of the proceeds goes to the National Alliance to End Homelessness.

**Pun** is an avid nightmare enjoyer and takes a great deal of inspiration from their vivid dreams. Their primary pastime is picking up new hobbies and getting lost in research spirals. They cultivated a love of literature and the macabre from a young age, and when they were eight they penned a poem about dancing with ghouls in a graveyard on the autumnal equinox which their fourth grade teacher found mildly concerning. Pun continued to pursue this passion throughout middle and high school, often at inappropriate times such as during class or while backstage at theatre rehearsals.

This focus on writing, as well as the desire to better understand the human psyche, led Pun to study both psychology and literature in university. They graduated from the University of Iowa in 2016 with dual degrees and continued their education by earning a Masters of Science in Psychology from Arizona State University in 2022. Their writing lends a great deal from psychology, centering on character interiority and physical manifestations of abstract concepts. They currently manage the Volunteer Services & YouthWorks department at the Discovery Children's Museum in Las Vegas, Nevada.

**Nat Reiher** is an author-in-progress whose wife convinced him to start submitting stuff. He has accomplished nothing. Nat writes under a pseudonym to keep his professional life (serious adult attorney) separate from his writing life (horror-obsessed degenerate). You can follow him @natreiher on Twitter to read all his bad takes.

**Luz Rosales** is a college student and horror lover from Los Angeles. They have been published in *Strange Horizons*, X-R-A-Y, *Witch Craft Magazine*, *Black Telephone Magazine*, and elsewhere. They were a 2022 *Lambda Literary* Fellow in the Speculative Fiction cohort. They can be found on Twitter @SPLITTER-CORES.

**Kaylee Rowena** (she/they) is a comic artist and illustrator haunting Baltimore, Maryland. She loves to tell ghost stories. You can find her at kayleerowena.com, or by shouting into the nearest haunted house and listening very closely for a response.

**J. M. Tyree** is the coauthor of the fiction collection *Our Secret Life in the Movies* (with Michael McGriff, *A Strange Object/Deep Vellum*), an NPR Best Books Selection. Tyree's short stories have appeared in *American Short Fiction*, ergot, *Guernica*, and *New England Review*. His uncanny novella, *The Haunted Screen*, is forthcoming from *A Strange Object/Deep Vellum*.

# Content warnings

Warnings are written by the authors and my not be exhaustive. Please note this anthology is about horror and is not suitable for children.

### Highway to Hell: Cars in Horror Cinema
Discussion of car accidents; brief reference to suicide

### Tachycardia
Violence; gore; medical emergencies

### The Greys
Disease; death

### Peach Pit
Insects (ants, moths, flies, maggots); nonviolent animal death; description of corpses (tadpoles, salamanders, raccoon, human); description of physical injury (mild blood); description of infection (tetanus); emeto; implied domestic violence

### Nobody Wants to Be Around You When You're Depressed
Suicide; self-harm; murder; child death; disordered eating

### Vampire Radio
Mental illness; morphine addiction; blood

9 798210 744975